PITCHERS

TWENTY-SEVEN OF BASEBALL'S GREATEST

George Sullivan

Atheneum 1994 New York

Maxwell Macmillan Canada
Toronto

Maxwell Macmillan International
New York Oxford Singapore Sydney

"BASEBALL CARD" PHOTOS COURTESY OF:
Wide World: 5, 8, 12, 14, 16, 20, 22, 24, 26, 28, 30, 32, 34, 40, 46, 52, 64
National Baseball Library: 36, 38, 48, 50, 56, 58, 60, 62, 68
Baseball Nostalgia: 44

Atheneum
Macmillan Publishing Company
866 Third Avenue
New York, NY 10022

Maxwell Macmillan Canada, Inc.
1200 Eglinton Avenue East
Suite 200
Don Mills, Ontario M3C 3N1

Macmillan Publishing Company is part of the Maxwell Communication Group of Companies.

First edition
Printed in the United States of America
10 9 8 7 6 5 4 3 2 1

Book production by Daniel Adlerman

Library of Congress Cataloging-in-Publication Data

Sullivan, George, 1927–
Pitchers / by George Sullivan.—1st ed.
p. cm.
Includes index.
Summary: Profiles twenty-seven of the best pitchers in the history of baseball, including Nolan Ryan, Tom Seaver, Whitey Ford, Dizzy Dean, and Cy Young.
ISBN 0-689-31825-1
1. Pitchers (Baseball)—United States—Biography—Juvenile literature. [1. Baseball players.] I. Title.
GV865.A1S86 1994
796.357'092'2—dc20
[B] 93-3007

Contents

Introduction

Good hitters win ball games. But a good pitcher can stop a good hitter cold.

This wasn't always so. In baseball's earliest days, the pitcher had to pitch underhand, feeding the ball to the batter merely as a means of putting it in play.

Pitching rules began to take on their modern form in the late 1800s. After much trial and error, the pitching distance was set at 60 feet, 6 inches, what it is today, in 1893. Three strikes have been an out since 1888, and four balls a walk since 1889.

But pitchers didn't really begin to get control of the game until after the turn of the century. In 1901, the National League decided a foul ball should be considered a strike, and the American League made the same ruling two years later. By increasing the likelihood of strikes versus balls, this change shifted the balance of power to the pitcher.

Still, during the early 1900s, baseball was different from what it is today. The strategy of most teams was to work toward one run at a time. Hitters were poke hitters. They sought to slap the ball through the infield for a single. A sacrifice or a stolen base to move that runner ahead usually followed. Teams were less likely to look for the "long ball" to score several runs at a time.

Red Murray of the New York Giants led the National League in home runs in 1909 with seven. Frank ("Home Run") Baker of the Philadelphia Athletics, the most noted slugger of his time, led the American League in homers for four consecutive years. He hit 11 in 1911, 10 in 1912, 12 in 1913, and 9 in 1914.

Because home runs were so rare, a pitcher could risk letting a batter put the ball in play. Consequently, he didn't have to throw hard on every pitch. He could pace himself, saving his best stuff for when there was a real threat.

In his book, *Pitching in a Pinch,* Christy Mathewson, who broke in with the Giants in 1900, noted that he had lost a game early in his career by giving up four runs in the ninth inning because he hadn't "saved his stuff." After the game, his manager told him, "Never mind, Matty. It was worth it. The game ought to teach you not to pitch your head off when you don't need to."

Wee Willie Keller, a star for Baltimore, Brooklyn, and then the New York Giants in the 1890s and early 1900s, was one of baseball's most successful poke hitters. *(Baseball Nostalgia)*

The fact that pitchers could hold back and conserve their energy is one reason that Cy Young and Walter Johnson and others were able to pitch so many more games than pitchers of the present day. They could pitch more frequently, with less rest, and it was easier to win 30 or even 40 games in a season, or 300 games in one's career. Pitchers threw hard, of course, but they threw *really* hard only 15 or 20 times a game.

Dramatic change came in the 1920s. The great Babe Ruth helped to trigger that change. He hit 54 home runs in 1920, when nobody else in the American League hit more than 19. He hit more runs that season than any other *team*. Within a few years, almost every other hitter was trying to do what Babe Ruth was doing, and many succeeded.

Before long, slugging records were being rewritten and runs scored reached historic levels. Babe Ruth wasn't the only reason. The outbreak of slugging also came about because in 1921 the spitball and "emery ball" were banned. No longer were pitchers able to deliberately scuff or add foreign substances to the ball. Clean new baseballs had to be served up to every hitter.

Some baseball historians credit the slugging explosion to the fact that the owners and manufacturers tinkered with the innards of the baseball, making the ball livelier. This was done, supposedly, by winding tighter the wool yarn that surrounds the ball's core, which would make the ball jump from the bat. This, in turn, would lead to more home runs and scoring, which the fans liked to see. The game itself would become livelier, and attendance figures would soar as a result.

Whatever the reason for it, the slugging epidemic changed baseball for all time. Pitching was transformed. No longer could a pitcher "save his stuff" for a key moment. A run could now be scored at any instant. Every batter was a threat. Every moment was a key moment.

Interestingly, the number of strikeouts also increased. After the early 1920s, many hitters, seeking to become home run heroes, favored "all or nothing" swings. They were easy prey for control pitchers, those who had learned to be precise and consistent in placing the ball where they wanted to place it.

Throughout these decades, a good pitcher was expected to finish any game he started. That idea, of course, has gone the way of poke hitters. What's happened is that relief specialists have become increasingly important.

The concept of having one pitcher enter the game to replace another goes back to baseball's earliest days, but it remained a little-used piece of strategy until fairly recently. In the 1890s, pitchers completed about 80 percent of the games they started.

In the late 1920s and during the 1930s, "star relief" was common. The ace of a team's staff would make 10 to 20 appearances a season at crucial moments. Lefty Grove, for example, saved 55 games during his career. Some teams had bullpen specialists, but they were mostly old starters, veterans who still knew how to pitch but no longer were up to the demands of being a member of a four- or five-man starting rotation.

The full-time relief ace didn't become a reality until the 1940s. One of the first was the New York Yankees' Joe Page, who saved a then record 27 games in 1949. Page was among the first pitchers used in a relief role on a day-in, day-out basis.

During the 1950s, every team seemed to feel the need for a Joe Page. The job kept growing in importance. During the 1970s, more career pitchers actually started as relievers, and starred as such. All the while, the idea that a starter had to finish what he started was fading.

Sparky Anderson, managing the Cincinnati Reds at the time, and Dick Williams, manager of the Oakland A's, helped to develop the relatively new idea of the "setup man." A new type of relief pitcher, he's the specialist who is brought in to protect a lead for two or three innings, preparing the way for the more traditional reliever known as the "stopper" or "closer."

The fact that the manager can use so many talented pitchers in one game has made hitting tougher. It used to be that a hitter would have two or three at bats to evaluate a pitcher. Nowadays that seldom happens. The hitter is always looking at an ace with a fresh arm.

Relief pitching's high-flying status was also reflected by pitching statistics. Complete games, for example, started becoming as obsolete as Sunday doubleheaders.

Another change was that workhorse pitchers began to fade from the scene. Pitchers who could and did pitch 300 innings in a season, such as Nolan Ryan, Bert Blyleven, Tom Seaver, and Gaylord Perry, played a valuable role, making the season much less of a chore for the other starters and taking pressure off the bullpen. But the last pitcher

Sparky Anderson helped develop the idea of pitching's "setup man." *(George Sullivan)*

to pitch 300 innings over the regular season was Steve Carlton of the Philadelphia Phillies in 1980.

At the same time relief pitching was growing in importance, pitchers were getting trickier. Up until the late 1940s, there were two basic pitches, the fastball and curve. Then the slider became popular. A pitch that looks like a fastball until it gets three or four feet from the hitter, then breaks just enough to throw him off stride or to miss the fat part of his bat, the slider "changed hitting entirely," said Ted Williams. By 1950, most of the best pitchers had mastered the slider.

Just as the slider was the pitch of the 1950s, so the split-fingered fastball was the pitch of the 1980s. Made popular by Bruce Sutter of the Chicago Cubs, a relief specialist who won the National League's Cy Young Award in 1979, the split-finger looks like a fastball when it leaves the pitcher's hand, but it has a forward rotation, like a curve, and breaks down hard and late. Rusty Staub, a onetime outfielder and later a broadcaster for the

New York Mets, said the split-finger makes "good pitchers into very good pitchers and very good pitchers into starters."

Throughout most of baseball history, the pitcher has had the advantage in his duel with the batter. He knows when he plans to release the ball and where he intends to throw it. He knows the type of pitch the batter is going to have to face—fastball, curve, slider, split-finger, or something else. He's provided with a hill—the "mound"—from which he hurls his pitches. The increased emphasis on relief pitching over the past couple of decades, the fact that the starter has become a part-timer, hasn't changed the pitcher's status. It has, in fact, tipped the scales more heavily in his favor.

This book profiles the best pitchers in baseball history. In part, at least, the players featured were chosen on the basis of pitching statistics. Earned run averages (ERAs) were particularly important. The best pitchers have the lowest ERA. There is no better indicator of a pitcher's ability.

Several other statistics are also meaningful. Winning percentage is important, of course, as is the number of walks a pitcher issues. Three walks for every nine-inning game isn't bad; less than three is good.

Walks can also be compared to strikeouts. Two strikeouts for every walk indicates good control. (Roger Clemens of the Boston Red Sox, during his first nine years in the majors, averaged between *three* and *four* strikeouts for every walk, which helps to explain his greatness.)

Of course, when it comes to pitching, there are other factors besides mechanical considerations and what appears in the box score. Pitching requires thinking. The pitcher has to have a clear idea of how to pitch to each hitter. This takes study and planning; it takes mental effort. "What happens in your head is probably as important as what goes on with your throwing arm," Nolan Ryan once said.

Today's pitchers are helped enormously by hitters who swing on impulse, without any clear idea of the strike zone. A pitcher could never get by on instinct alone.

The pitchers selected here also have shown some staying power, the ability to excel for more than a few seasons. There have been pitchers such as Don Larsen of the Yankees, who, on October 8, 1956, pitched the first World Series no-hitter, the first Series perfect game, and the sixth perfect game in the modern era of baseball. Few recall what Larsen, as a pitcher, did before or after that game. He was a one-day sensation.

Other pitchers have been superstars for brief periods. Denny McLain, who won 31 games in 1968, and Jack Chesbro, a 41-game winner in 1904, are two examples.

To have a pitching career that stretches for a decade or more takes great talent, of course, plus good health and a refusal to quit. Nolan Ryan, Steve Carlton, and Warren Spahn went on and on, driven more by pride than by a paycheck.

Thousands of pitchers have dazzled major league fans over the past century. The best are real artists. There is beauty in their creations. These are their stories.

Denny McLain, a 31-game winner for the Tigers in 1968 *(Detroit Tigers)*

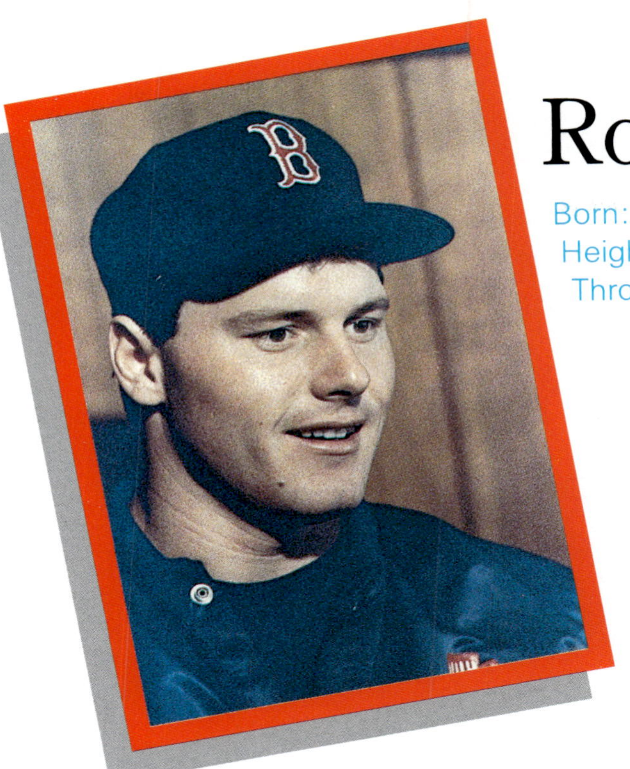

Roger Clemens

Born: August 4, 1962; Dayton, Ohio
Height: 6′4″ Weight: 220
Throws right-handed, bats right-handed

He's an awesome power pitcher with a 94-mile-an-hour fastball that he can throw when he wants, a good curve, and exceptional control. There are days he is almost untouchable, absolutely the best pitcher in baseball. He's won the Cy Young Award three times in eight years (some of those with injuries) and set an all-time record by striking out 20 batters in a nine-inning game.

But Roger Clemens of the Red Sox has also been described as a hotheaded troublemaker. His behavior during one game of the American League Championship Series in 1990 earned him more headlines than any of his pitching feats.

As a young teenager growing up on the outskirts of Houston, Roger's hero was all-time strikeout leader Nolan Ryan, a Texas neighbor. In just a few seasons of major league competition, Clemens bloomed as Ryan's rival as baseball's most dominant pitcher. He's been called a "Ryan with an attitude."

Drafted originally by the Mets after a season at San Jacinto Junior College, Roger chose to pitch for the University of Texas instead of signing with the New York team. In 1983, he pitched the team to the college baseball championship.

Drafted by the Red Sox that June, Roger was assigned to Winter Haven (Florida) in the Class A Florida State League, but was quickly advanced to

By the age of 30, Clemens had won the Cy Young Award three times. *(L. G. Balfour Co.)*

Clemens has excellent control, a good curve, and a 94-mile-an-hour fastball. *(Wide World)*

Clemens talks to reporters after agreeing to a three-year, $7.5 million contract, which made him the highest-paid pitcher in baseball history. *(Wide World)*

AA competition at New Britain (Connecticut) in the Eastern League. Early the next season, he was promoted to the Red Sox roster.

Roger had a better-than-average rookie season, winning nine, losing four. But in 1985, shoulder problems kept him on the disabled list for long stretches. Surgery was required before the season ended.

As the 1986 season began, Roger's shoulder was still a cause for concern. He quickly stilled the club's fears, winning his first three starts. On April 29 that year, he turned in one of the finest pitching performances in major league history, with 20 strikeouts in a 3–1 win over the Seattle Mariners. At one stage during the game, Clemens struck out eight batters in a row, tying a league record. He did not issue a single base on balls.

The next day, when Roger entered the Boston clubhouse, he saw a sign posted over his locker. ROCKET MAN, it read. That became Roger's nickname.

Clemens ended the season with a 24–4 record and a 2.48 earned run average. He captured the Cy Young and Most Valuable Player Awards. But in postseason competition, the Rocket fizzled, winning only one of four starts. The Red Sox dropped the World Series to the Mets in seven games.

Clemens had a second 20-game season in 1987, finishing with a 20–9 record, and won his second Cy Young Award. He is only the fourth pitcher in history to win the award in back-to-back seasons.

Roger has a passion for keeping physically fit. He has six different exercise machines at his home in Framingham outside Boston. In the mornings, he sometimes runs on the streets of his neighborhood. In the afternoons, he often can be seen running on the streets near Fenway Park.

"Roger Clemens's commitment to personal conditioning is unmatched by anyone I've ever known in this business," Dr. Arthur Pappas, the Boston Red Sox physician, once told *Sports Illustrated.* "If I were to suggest anything to him that would help, he would do it exactly. If I told him that standing in a corner for 12 hours with a silly hat on his head would help, he'd stand in the corner for 12 hours with the hat."

In 1990, with a 21–6 mark and a 1.93 earned run average, the best in the league, Roger helped the Red Sox win the Eastern Division title again. In the playoffs, the Sox faced the Oakland A's, who won the first three games.

Despite a tender shoulder, Roger started the fourth game, hoping to prevent an Oakland sweep. In the second inning, he got into a heated dispute with umpire Terry Cooney over a pitch the umpire called a ball. Cooney accused Clemens of cursing at him and threw him out of the game. No pitcher had ever been thrown out of a playoff game before. The messy incident got more attention than Oakland's 3–1 victory that ended the season for the Red Sox.

Clemens was in the headlines again early the next year when he signed a $21.5 million contract extension, which made him, at 28, the highest-paid player in baseball history. Clemens won the third of his Cy Young Awards that season.

"Two qualities make Clemens rare among power pitchers," Nolan Ryan once observed. "First, his fastball explodes down in the strike zone. Second, there's his control. The only others who could match him were Koufax at the end of his career and Bob Gibson."

By the age of 30, Roger Clemens had already made his mark. He owned the record for strikeouts in a game. He was the youngest pitcher to win three Cy Young Awards. He is almost certain to break the records of a great many pitchers, Nolan Ryan among them.

As a youngster, Clemens, who idolized Nolan Ryan, never dreamed he'd play in the majors with him. Now he's breaking his records. *(Wide World)*

Nolan Ryan

Born: January 31, 1947; Refugio, Texas
Height: 6′2″ Weight: 212
Throws right-handed, bats right-handed

He's the greatest power pitcher in the history of baseball, an ageless flamethrower who reigns as baseball's strikeout king and the only man to pitch seven no-hitters. (No other pitcher has more than four.) As he began his twenty-seventh major league season in 1993 at the age of 46, Nolan Ryan was still able to overpower batters by hurling fastballs at speeds of over 90 miles an hour.

Fastballers are supposed to break down, lose their speed, start relying on curves or gimmicks to make the baseball do funny things. Not Nolan Ryan. He attained the incredible milestone of 5,000 strikeouts at the age of 42. There can be no denying that Ryan is a physical wonder, a pitcher who, as a sheer athlete, is in a class by himself.

As the 1993 season got under way, Ryan held more than three dozen major records, including a total of 5,668 strikeouts. He had 319 victories against 287 losses and a lifetime 3.14 earned run average.

Nolan Ryan grew up in Alvin, Texas, outside of Houston, where his wife, Ruth, and their three teenage children live today. In high school, Nolan became known for his unhittable fastball—and lack of control.

The Mets selected Nolan in the 1965 free-agent draft. At Greenville (South Carolina) in the Western Carolinas League in 1966, he frightened batters and catchers alike with his scorching fastball. He also won 17 games. At the end of the season, he was called up by the Mets, a team that had finished last or next to last every year since the team was formed in 1962.

New York City held no charms for Nolan and he was often homesick. He missed much of the 1967 season because of an arm injury and service with the Army Reserve.

Things improved in 1968. Nolan married his high school sweetheart, which helped to cure his homesickness. Tom Seaver and Jerry Koosman joined the pitching staff, positioning the Mets for their truly amazing turnaround in 1969. Nine and a half games behind the Cubs in August, the team closed with a rush to win the pennant.

Manager Gil Hodges didn't quite know what to do with Ryan that season, and used him both as a starter and a reliever. He finished the season with a 6–3 record. But with seven innings of relief he won the deciding game in the league championship series and saved the third game of the World Series, as the miracle Mets upset the Baltimore Orioles in five games. Ryan called winning the World Series a once-in-a-lifetime feeling, adding, "I've spent the rest of my career trying to rediscover it."

Ryan struggled through the next two seasons. Still unhappy with life in New York City, he asked the Mets to trade him. They did. Late in 1971, the Mets sent Ryan and three other players to the California Angels in exchange for third baseman Jim Fregosi. The trade is often cited as the worst in Mets history.

Ryan was happy when he was traded to the Astros because it meant returning to his native Texas. *(Wide World)*

Ryan spent four sometimes gloomy seasons with the Mets before being traded. *(George Sullivan)*

With the Angels, pitching with a more compact delivery, Ryan began to win superstar status. In 1972, with a 19–16 record and 329 strikeouts, he became the first right-hander since Bob Feller to fan 300 or more batters in a season, a feat Feller accomplished in 1946.

Ryan was even more overpowering the next year. He struck out 383 hitters, the all-time record for a season, while becoming the first pitcher with back-to-back 300-strikeout seasons. And Ryan became only the fifth pitcher in history to toss two no-hitters in a season. The first came on May 15, 1973, against the Kansas City Royals, the second on July 15 against the Detroit Tigers. In his next start, he was six outs from yet another no-hitter when the streak was stopped.

Ryan made it three seasons in a row of 300-or-more strikeouts when he fanned 367 in 1974. He also pitched his third no-hitter. His fourth came in 1975.

After undergoing elbow surgery in 1975, Ryan came back as good as ever. He was 17–18 with

One of baseball's hardest-firing pitchers, Ryan is only the twentieth to win 300 games. *(Texas Rangers)*

327 strikeouts in 1976 and 19–16 with 341 strikeouts in 1977.

Ryan became a free agent at the end of 1979, then signed a three-year contract with the Houston Astros. In so doing, he became baseball's first million-dollar-a-year pitcher. It wasn't just the money that was important to Ryan. The contract also meant he finally would be returning to his native Texas.

It took a while for Ryan to get adjusted to pitching in the National League again. But by 1981 he was back in top form, leading the league with a 1.69 earned run average. He also pitched his fifth no-hitter that year.

The seasons of 1984 and 1985 were marred by injury, and twice in 1986 Ryan was on the disabled list with a tender elbow. And although he passed his fortieth birthday in January 1987, he wasn't ready for retirement. "I know he'll be out there fighting," said Houston first baseman Glenn Davis not long before the 1987 season opened. "I don't care what the odds are."

Even Davis must have been surprised by Ryan's performance that year. His 2.76 earned run average enabled him to win his second ERA title. He led the league with 270 strikeouts and became the only pitcher in history with 2,000 strikeouts in each league.

Ryan became a free agent in 1988, then signed with the Texas Rangers. With the Rangers, Ryan was as unhittable as ever. In his first two years with the team, he led the league in strikeouts. He had his sixth no-hitter in 1990.

Ryan's seventh no-hitter, against the Toronto Blue Jays, came in 1991. He started the game with only four days' rest so he would be pitching before the home crowd on Arlington Appreciation Night. (Arlington, Texas, is where the Rangers are based.) He struck out 16 that night. Roberto Alomar was the game's final out. His father, Sandy Alomar, was the second baseman for the Angels when Ryan pitched the first two of his no-hitters.

Ryan was to strikeouts what Hank Aaron was to home runs, and his name dominates the record book. At the beginning of the season of 1993, these were some of the records he held:

- Most strikeouts, career—5,668
- Most strikeouts, season—383, California Angels, 1973
- Most years, 100 or more strikeouts—25
- Most years, 200 or more strikeouts—15
- Most years, 300 or more strikeouts—6
- Most consecutive strikeouts, game, American League—8, California Angels, July 9, 1972 and August 7, 1973

Twice in his career, Ryan fanned three batters in one inning on just nine pitched balls. That's pitching perfection. He did it with the Mets in 1968 and with the Angels in 1972.

Ryan kind of shrugs when he is asked about some of his recent records, his 300th win or his 5,000th strikeout, for example. "They were attainable if I lasted long enough," he says.

He feels differently about the seventh no-hitter. That was a case, he says, where he "defied time."

RIGHT: Ryan in action against the Toronto Blue Jays on May 1, 1991, when he pitched his seventh no-hitter *(Wide World)*

BELOW: Ryan is carried off the field by his teammates after throwing his seventh no-hitter. *(Wide World)*

Bert Blyleven

Born: April 6, 1951; Zeist, Holland
Height: 6′3″ Weight: 220
Throws right-handed, bats right-handed

Boasting one of the nastiest curveballs in the game, Bert Blyleven carved out an exceptional career that covered more than two decades. Despite spending most of his best years with poor or mediocre teams, Blyleven, during the early 1990s, seemed certain to become the 21st pitcher to reach 300 victories.

His career victory total wasn't Blyleven's only noteworthy statistic. In 1992, with his 3,641st strikeout, Blyleven eased past Tom Seaver into third place on the career strikeout list. Only Nolan Ryan and Steve Carlton had struck out more.

Blyleven is also important because he was a workhorse. A pitcher that can give a team 250 to 300 innings in a season is a tremendous asset and, as mentioned earlier, less common today than in baseball's early days. He helps to take the pressure off other members of the pitching staff, making them more effective. Six times in his career, Blyleven pitched more than 275 innings during a season, with a high of 325 innings in 1973.

If there was any secret to Blyleven's success, it was starting young and staying around a long time. He was 19 years old when he made his major league debut with the Minnesota Twins on June 5, 1970.

Serious arm injuries came close to ending his career a number of times. He was traded five times. He once admitted to drug problems. But Blyleven endured. In 1992, he won his 280th game after missing almost two season with a torn rotator cuff. "To me age has never been a factor," said the 41-year-old Blyleven after the game. "I still feel like I'm in my late twenties."

When Blyleven joined the Minnesota Twins, his first major league club, in 1970, the aging team was on a downhill slide. Yet despite the lack of strong teams behind him, Blyleven had five seasons in which he had 15 or more wins and six seasons with 200 or more strikeouts. In 1973, he was 20–17 for the third-place Twins, his only 20-victory season.

Blyleven was traded to the Rangers in 1976. The following year he pitched a no-hitter against the Angels, winning, 6–0. When the Rangers dealt him to the Pittsburgh Pirates in 1978, Blyleven finally got to play for a winning team. He helped the Pirates win the World Series in 1979, contributing a victory in game five.

Blyleven's complaints the next year that he was being underused helped to get him traded to Cleveland. His solid performances in the season that followed tend to prove that he was right. He had a 19–7 record with the sixth-place Indians in 1984.

Blyleven found himself back in Minnesota in 1987. But this Minnesota team was much different. Bert won 15 and lost 12 during the regular season and then won two games in the league championship series and another in the World Series over the St. Louis Cardinals.

As his career went on and on, Blyleven continued to accumulate wins and strikeouts. The home runs he gave up grew in number, too. He surrendered 50 homers in 1986, a major league record. Pitching in the Metrodome, a heaven on earth for home run hitters, was a factor. Equally important, Blyleven was a control pitcher. When his wicked curve wasn't quite wicked enough, there was a good chance the ball would go sailing over the fence.

Blyleven moved to the Angels, his sixth team, in 1989. *(Wide World)*

Only Nolan Ryan and Steve Carlton have more strikeouts than Blyleven. *(Wide World)*

Blyleven moved to the Angels, his sixth team, in 1989. There he posted a 17–5 record, with a 2.73 earned run average, fourth best in the major leagues. He had five shutouts that season.

Blyleven finished the season of 1992 as the American League active career leader in victories and losses (due in part to the quality of the teams with which he played), strikeouts, shutouts, and innings pitched, and a bunch of other categories. Early in 1993, he returned to the Twins for a third time. His ambition, of course, was to win that 300th game.

Steve Carlton

Born: December 22, 1944; Miami, Florida
Height: 6′4″ Weight: 210
Threw left-handed, batted left-handed
Eligible for the Hall of Fame in 1994

Every era has its outstanding left-hander. In the 1920s and 1930s, it was Lefty Grove. In the late 1940s and 1950s, there was Warren Spahn. Sandy Koufax starred in the 1960s. In more recent years, the dominant lefty was Steve Carlton.

Carlton, who retired in 1988, won 329 games, second only to Spahn among left-handers. He had 4,136 strikeouts, more than any other pitcher except Nolan Ryan. He is the only pitcher in history to win four Cy Young Awards.

Carlton loved to pitch. That's where he put his time and energy. He didn't care much for socializing or public attention. When he pitched the clinching game in Philadelphia's World Series victory over Kansas City in 1980, Carlton sipped the traditional champagne in the trainer's room to escape the uproar of the clubhouse. And for almost half of his career, he was Silent Steve, refusing to grant interviews or even talk with reporters or broadcasters.

When Carlton had his first professional tryout in 1963, he failed to impress the scouts. They felt he couldn't throw hard enough. So Carlton went to work, building himself up with a weight-training program.

Before long, Carlton had a superior fastball and a decent curve. He also had one of the best pickoff moves in the game. After a couple of years of being shuttled back and forth between the Cards and the minor leagues, he joined St. Louis for good in 1967.

Carlton's first two seasons were respectable, but he really began to impress people in 1969, after he developed his nasty slider. It bewildered batters because it looked like his fastball until the last second, when it would break and drop. In a game against the Mets that year, he struck out a record 19 batters. (Roger Clemens of the Red Sox broke the record in 1986; Clemens struck out 20.)

Carlton and the Cards often quarreled over contracts. He missed spring training in 1970 because of such a dispute. After he won 20 games in 1971 and asked for a raise, the Cardinals turned him down. Instead, they traded him to the Phillies for pitcher Rick Wise. The trade ranks as one of the best deals in Philadelphia Phillies history.

Some pitching records look to be unbreakable.

Cy Young's 511 career wins, for example. Jack Chesbro's 41 victories in 1904 is another. Carlton also holds a record that will probably last for all time. In 1972, he pitched 15 consecutive victories for a last-place team, the Phillies. He finished the season with 27 of the team's 59 wins.

Carlton won the first of his four Cy Young Awards that year. He is the only pitcher ever to have won a Cy Young with a team that finished in last place.

Carlton had four more seasons in which he won 20 or more games, giving him a total of six. In 1980, with a 24–9 mark, he helped the Phillies win their first world championship. Carlton captured two games in the World Series, including the sixth and deciding game.

As a member of the Phillies, Carlton won 20 or more games six times. *(Wide World)*

Carlton in action against the Kansas City Royals in the 1980 World Series *(Wide World)*

Carlton began to falter in 1983. While he managed to lead the league in strikeouts for the fifth time, he lost more games than he won. In 1985, after he had a 1–8 record and spent much of the season on the disabled list, the Phillies asked him to retire. When he refused, the club released him.

Carlton believed his arm was sound and that he could still win ball games. He drifted from the San Francisco Giants to the Chicago White Sox, and then to the Indians and finally to the Twins, adding 11 victories to his total while losing 21. He delivered his last pitch in 1988.

Hitters rejoiced at his retirement. "Hitting against Steve Carlton," Willie Stargell once remarked, "was like trying to sip coffee through a fork."

Tom Seaver

Born: November 17, 1944; Fresno, California
Height: 6′1″ Weight: 210
Threw right-handed, batted right-handed
Elected to the Hall of Fame in 1992

Intelligent, hardworking Tom Seaver, the cover boy of the New York Mets, was a pitcher's pitcher. He pushed off the mound and delivered the ball with one fluid motion, with no lunging or falling back at the end of his delivery. From start to finish, everything was smooth and controlled. That peerless delivery produced one of the game's liveliest fastballs. As it neared the plate, it exploded. Like Steve Carlton, Roger Clemens, or Dwight Gooden in his prime, Seaver, with that fastball, could blow hitters away.

That wasn't all. As Nolan Ryan, his teammate on the Mets for four seasons, once noted, Seaver had "baseball smarts." He was crafty and analytical, able to get the very most from his baseball skills.

With the New York team, Seaver established himself as "Tom Terrific" and "The Franchise," the best pitcher ever to wear a Mets uniform. He holds the club record for starts, victories, complete games, innings pitched, shutouts, and strikeouts.

When he was elected to the Hall of Fame in 1992, he set yet another record. He was named on 425 of the 435 ballots, a 98.8 percentage, the highest in the history of the voting.

George Thomas Seaver was born in Fresno, California, and grew up there, the youngest of four children. He was a good player in Little League competition, but no standout. "I was a shrimp in those days," he once told Ira Berkow of the *New York Times*. "I needed all the power I could muster to throw the ball." That led to his compact and powerful knee-dragging pitching style. Being small was "a blessing in disguise," he said.

During a six-month stay in the Marine Corps after high school, Seaver shot up from 5-foot-7 and 160 pounds to 6-foot-1 and 200 pounds. At Fresno City College, he pitched for the school team. He pitched so well that he was offered a scholarship to the University of Southern California. After starring for a season at USC, Seaver was signed by the Mets in 1966. A season at Jacksonville (Florida) in the International League followed. Then Seaver was called up to the Mets.

Founded in 1962, the Mets were one of the sorriest teams in baseball. In 1966, the year before he joined the team, the Mets had finished ninth in the 10-team National League, some 48½ games behind the pennant-winning Los Angeles Dodgers. It was a young team developing a solid tradition for losing.

But Seaver wouldn't accept that. He was the National League's Rookie of the Year in 1967 and a 16-game winner in each of his first two seasons with the team. Said Nolan Ryan: "He was so good, so confident, so removed from whatever the Mets had been before, he became a symbol of the new breed, the better times looming."

In 1968, Gil Hodges took over as manager of the Mets. A proven leader, honest and direct with the players, Hodges was to have an important influence upon Seaver. "He was a pro's pro," Seaver said. "He taught me how to be a professional."

With the Mets, Seaver was known as "Tom Terrific." *(George Sullivan)*

Hodges and Seaver helped to make the Mets a team to be taken seriously. In 1969, the team dueled the Chicago Cubs for the Eastern Division championship. Seaver was brilliant in the Mets' sizzling stretch drive. He beat the Pirates with a neat six-hitter, 5–2; shut out the Montreal Expos, 2–0; and downed the Cards, 3–1. He won 25 games and lost only 7.

The Mets nosed out the Cubs for the division title and then defeated the Atlanta Braves in the league championship series. In the World Series against the favored Baltimore Orioles, the Met magic continued to prevail. The Orioles won the first game, defeating Seaver, 4–1. But that was the only game they won.

Tom won the fourth game, 2–1 in 10 innings. He was in the on-deck circle when J. C. Martin bunted and pinch runner Rod Gaspar raced home with the winning run. "I had always had this boyhood dream of winning a World Series," Seaver said, "and now I was standing there and seeing it happen right in front of me. It flashed before my eyes—a World Series winner!" That season Seaver captured the first of his three Cy Young Awards.

What was perhaps Seaver's most powerful pitching performance came the next year, 1970, in a game against the San Diego Padres. Seaver, with 19 strikeouts, tied Steve Carlton's record for strikeouts in a nine-inning game. (The record was later raised to 20 by Roger Clemens.) Seaver struck out a major league record ten straight batters in that game.

Seaver was 20–10 in 1971, 21–12 in 1972, and 19–10 in 1973 when the Mets were back in the World Series. This time there were no miracles. The Mets fell to the Oakland A's in seven games.

The years that followed were not always happy. A sore hip led to a mediocre season in 1974. His record slipped to 11–11, while his ERA shot up to 3.20. It was the first time his ERA had ever gone over 3.00.

But Seaver bounced back in 1975. His 22–9 record enabled him to lead the league in wins and winning percentage. He also led in strikeouts. He captured his third Cy Young Award that year.

Meanwhile, Seaver was having problems with the Met management. During 1976, he and M. Donald Grant, the club's general manager, quarreled both in private and in the press about Seaver's salary and the way things were being run.

Although he was upset with the club, Seaver was bitterly disappointed when the New York team abruptly traded him to the Reds in 1977. He had won 189 games for the team. He had looked forward to spending his entire career in a Mets uniform.

Yet later he felt differently about the trade. "It was good for me in that I got out of a bad situation," he said. "And it was good for the Mets. They were in disarray and soon they got new management."

As a member of the Reds, Seaver pitched the only no-hitter of his career—a 4–0 win over the Cardinals in 1978.

Seaver won his 300th game in 1985 at Yankee Stadium, pitching for the Chicago White Sox. *(Wide World)*

Seaver returned to the Mets for a brief stay in 1983. A year later he was obtained by the Chicago White Sox, who, in turn, dealt him to the Boston Red Sox. He finished his 20-year career with the Red Sox in 1986.

Seaver ended with a 311–205 record, 3,640 strikeouts, which, after being surpassed by Bert Blyleven in 1992, still ranks as the fourth highest total in history, and a 2.85 earned run average, the seventh best in history. He won three Cy Young Awards—in 1969, 1973, and 1975.

Seaver is jubilant as a fly ball by the Yankees' Don Baylor is caught to end the game that earned him his 300th win. *(Wide World)*

Seaver ended his career as a member of the Boston Red Sox. *(Wide World)*

One other set of statistics gives evidence of all that he accomplished. At an auction of Hall of Fame memorabilia in New York in 1992, Seaver's 1969 pin-striped Mets jersey was purchased by a collector for $50,000. A jacket that Seaver wore from 1967 to 1969 brought $10,000. A partly chewed toothpick from a pocket in the jacket sold for $400. Now that's an indication of real greatness.

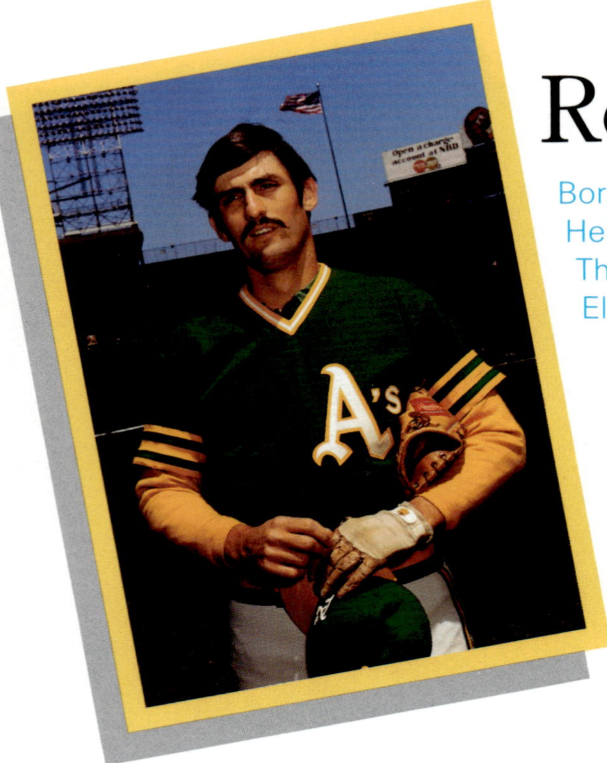

Rollie Fingers

Born: August 25, 1946; Steubenville, Ohio
Height: 6′4″ Weight: 190
Threw right-handed, batted right-handed
Elected to the Hall of Fame in 1992

Rollie Fingers is the only pitcher in the Hall of Fame who lost more games than he won. When he wrapped up his 17-year major league career in 1985, he had a 114–118 lifetime record.

But no one pays any attention to that statistic. That's because Fingers was a relief pitcher, perhaps the best of all time, the pitcher who brought dignity to the role. As is the case with any reliever, Fingers's accomplishments are recorded in saves, awarded when a pitcher is successful in preserving a victory by protecting his team's lead.

Almost as famous for his waxed handlebar mustache as for his pitching, the tall and lanky Fingers starred with the Oakland A's in their glory years—the early to mid-1970s, when the club won five division championships, three pennants, and three world championships. Fingers left the A's following the season of 1976 for the Padres and then through another trade became a member of the Milwaukee Brewers.

In the strike-shortened season of 1981, Fingers developed a forkball to go with his sinking fastball and hard slider. He was never better, pitching the Brewers into postseason competition. The team was ousted by the Yankees in the five-game Eastern Division playoff, despite a win and save by Fingers.

That season, Fingers led the American League in saves with 28 and was a factor in 55 percent of Milwaukee's victories. He won the league's Most Valuable Player Award and the Cy Young Award, becoming the first relief pitcher to win both in the same season. Of course, he was also named Reliever of the Year.

Fingers's record in World Series competition is just as impressive as his record in regular season play. In the 1973 Series between the Oakland A's and the Los Angeles Dodgers, Fingers ended up with a win, two saves, a 1.93 earned run average, and a new car as the Most Valuable Player in the Series. In all he pitched six saves across three World Series.

Rollie's career almost came to an end before it got started. While pitching for Birmingham (Alabama) in the Southern League in 1967, a line drive fractured his jaw and cheekbone. Fingers recovered from the mishap and went on to enjoy two successful seasons at Birmingham. He joined the A's late in 1968.

Fingers had problems at first. As a member of the A's starting rotation, he had trouble with the pressure. The night before he was assigned to start, he would toss and turn, unable to sleep. The next day he'd be exhausted by the fourth or fifth inning.

As a solution to the problem, the A's switched him to the bullpen. That appealed to him. He liked the idea of storming in to put down a rally. And since he never knew until the last minute when he was going to be used, there was no tension. By 1971, he was a full-time fireman, respected for his sinking fastball and, later, a hard slider.

Following his outstanding season in 1981, Fingers had injury problems for several years. Nevertheless, when he decided to end his career in 1985, Fingers had saved a record 341 games. In 1992, the record was topped by Jeff Reardon of the Red Sox in a game against the Yankees at Fenway Park. But saves nowadays are cheaper than they were in Fingers's time. That's because baseball's rules committee changed the definition of a save, making saves easier to achieve.

Jeff Reardon would be the first to admit that. Interviewed immediately after breaking Fingers's record, Reardon said, "Rollie Fingers was the best reliever ever. He always will be the best, no matter what I do."

A member of the Brewers staff, Fingers winds up during the first day of spring training in 1981. *(Wide World)*

Jim Palmer

Born: October 15, 1945; New York, New York
Height: 6′3″ Weight: 195
Threw right-handed, batted right-handed
Elected to the Hall of Fame in 1990

Jim Palmer's teammates on the Orioles called him "Cakes" because he liked to eat pancakes whenever he was due to pitch. The diet must have worked, because the handsome, high-kicking right-hander was one of the most durable and dependable of all pitchers. In his 19-year career, Palmer won 20 or more games eight times and was a three-time Cy Young Award winner.

A high fastball pitcher, who was almost unhittable once he found his groove, Palmer spent his entire career with the Orioles, becoming the best hurler in the team's history. Signed in 1963, he toiled for two years in the minors and finally joined the Baltimore starting rotation in 1966. And he started fast.

As a rookie, he led the club with 15 wins. In the World Series that fall, nine days away from his twenty-first birthday, Palmer became the youngest pitcher in history to record a Series shutout, as he defeated Sandy Koufax and the Dodgers in game two.

But dark days followed. Arm, back, and shoulder problems almost ended his career. For two years, Palmer struggled, pitching in the minor leagues, trying to work his way back.

Finally, thanks to surgery and hard work, Palmer was able to pitch again at a high level. Four days after coming off the disabled list in 1969, he fired a no-hitter against the Oakland A's. He had a 16–4 record that year. In 1970, he recorded the first of eight seasons in which he won 20 or more victories. Only two other American League pitchers had as many 20-win seasons as Palmer—Walter Johnson, with 12, and Lefty Grove, with 8.

Palmer managed to be durable and dependable despite the fact that, after injuring his arm early in his career, he almost always pitched in pain. "Pain was pretty much a part of my pitching for the last 15 or 16 years," he once said.

In 1973, with an earned run average of 2.40, Palmer won the first of his two ERA titles. With a 2.09 ERA in 1975, he claimed his second title. Palmer won the Cy Young Award in 1973, 1975, and 1976. Only Steve Carlton, with four, has more.

Many pitchers have had better seasons than Palmer's best. But only a very few have had so many years at the top. Palmer's long reign was no accident. He worked hard to stay in shape. "If you're serious about it," he said, "you're going to stay as well conditioned as you can."

One of Palmer's routines was to play tennis at midday, when it was hot and humid. He believed it was good for building his stamina.

Palmer, arguably baseball's best pitcher of the 1970s, started the 1980s with a 16–10 record. He was 7–8 in 1981 and 15–5 in 1982. His last victory came at the age of 39 in a relief role in the third game of the 1983 World Series, won by the Orioles. He ended his career with a total of 268 regular season wins and 152 losses, which make for an excellent .638 percentage.

Palmer went on to become a successful baseball broadcaster and model for Jockey underwear. In 1991, at 45, he attempted a comeback with the Orioles. Money may have been one reason. The most Palmer ever earned in a season was $600,000. Roger Clemens of the Red Sox was earning that much in a month.

In his debut, a spring training game against the Red Sox, Palmer was hit hard, and he gave up the comeback try. Broadcasting and modeling seemed much easier.

ABOVE: Palmer pitches against the Boston Red Sox in his 1991 comeback attempt. *(Wide World)*

LEFT: Palmer and former Cincinnati second baseman Joe Morgan pose for photographers following their election to the Baseball Hall of Fame in 1990. *(Wide World)*

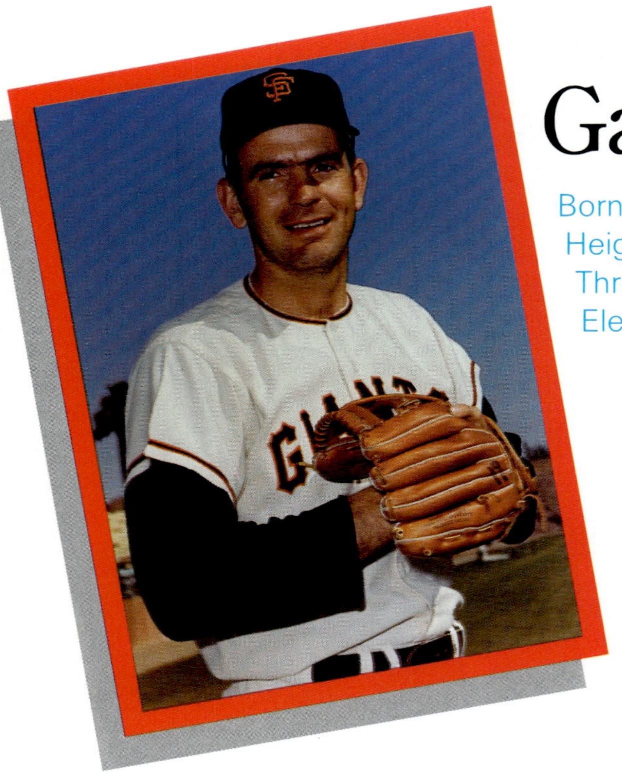

Gaylord Perry

Born: September 15, 1938; Williamston, North Carolina
Height: 6′4″ Weight: 215
Threw right-handed, batted right-handed
Elected to the Hall of Fame in 1991

The only pitcher to win the Cy Young Award in both the American and National Leagues, and the winner of 314 games, Gaylord Perry was the subject of hot debate throughout his long career, and even after he retired in 1982 at the age of 45. The reason: He was suspected of breaking the rules established in 1921 prohibiting tampering with the baseball, whether it was by applying saliva, Vaseline, or some other type of grease.

The method behind such tactics is to lubricate the fingers enough to be able to kind of squirt the ball toward the plate with no spin. The ball behaves like a knuckleball, dancing and darting, but is easier than a knuckler to control.

Baseball outlawed the spitter in 1921. In 1968, the rule makers went a step further, making it illegal for a pitcher to touch his mouth with his pitching hand while on the mound.

For breaking these rules, a pitcher is charged with a ball on the first illegal pitch and warned. If he continues to violate the rules, he can be ejected.

On the mound, Perry was constantly putting the rules to a test. He never stopped fidgeting, touching his face, his glove, different parts of his uniform, and tugging at the bill of his cap.

And the strategy worked. As Fran Healy, who caught for Perry and batted against him, once said: "I don't think he threw the spitter as much as everybody thought. But even when he didn't throw it, it worked for him, because of the anxiety it created."

Because he got people to believe he was tampering with the ball, the umpires were always checking Perry's hands, neck, ears, and hair. They examined and made him change various parts of his uniform. Joe Cronin, the president of the American League, once had a chemist analyze baseballs that Perry had thrown. No substance was found.

When asked whether he threw the spitter, Perry would simply grin. All he wanted was for the batters to think he did.

Perry's career began on a high note in 1958 when he signed a $90,000 contract with the San Francisco Giants. Four years in the minor leagues followed.

Once he did join the Giants, Perry pitched in the

shadow of the team's great right-hander, Juan Marichal. But he began to compete with Marichal for the spotlight in 1966 when he posted a 21–8 record.

In 1968, Perry pitched a no-hitter against the Cards. In 1970, with a 23–13 record, he led the National League in victories. Perry won the first of his Cy Young Awards in 1972.

Traded to the Cleveland Indians, Perry was quick to show he could be as successful in the American League as he had been in the National. He won 24 games for the fifth-place Indians in 1972, becoming the league leader in victories.

In 1975 Perry was dealt to the Texas Rangers, who traded him back to the National League. With the Padres in 1978, at the age of 40, Perry compiled a 21–6 record and won his second Cy Young Award. It was the fifth season in which he had won 20 or more games.

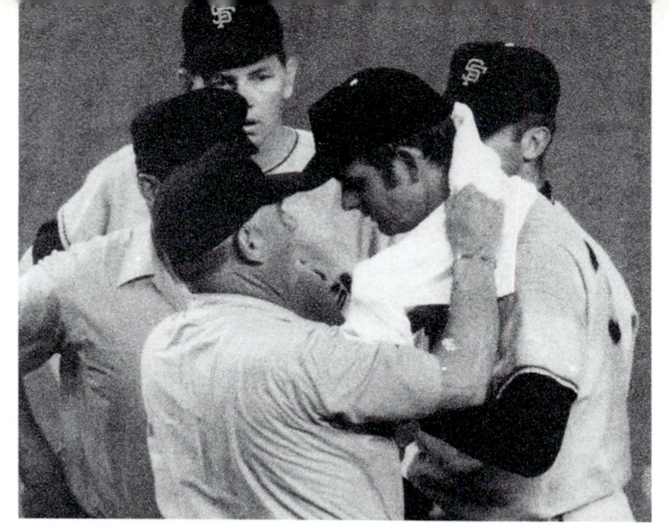

Umpire Paul Pryor wipes Perry's neck after finding some kind of substance there during a game in 1970, with Perry pitching for the Giants against the Astros. *(Wide World)*

Perry was pitching for the Seattle Mariners when he won his 300th game in 1982. *(Seattle Mariners)*

Perry was pitching for Atlanta in 1981 and was three wins short of the 300-victory mark when the club released him. To get a chance at that mark with the Seattle Mariners, Perry had to agree to a big pay cut. His payoff came in the record books when he won his 300th game in 1982.

The following year, as a member of the Kansas City Royals, Perry wrapped up his career at the age of 45. In 22 years, he won 314 games. His 3,534 strikeouts were second on the all-time list. Despite his many individual achievements, Perry played on only one division championship team.

After retiring, Perry wrote his autobiography, titled *Me and the Spitter.* In it he revealed that he did indeed throw more than a few greaseballs during his 22-season career, but mostly when he needed a big out or a strikeout.

After Perry's 300th win, outfielder Dave Winfield of the Yankees summed up what many players felt when he said, "You get by with what you can get by with in life. Nobody will put an asterisk on his victories. All you can do is give him credit." The truth or falsity of that statement is up to each of us to judge.

Bob Gibson

Born: November 9, 1935; Omaha, Nebraska
Height: 6′1″ Weight: 195
Threw right-handed, batted right-handed
Elected to the Hall of Fame in 1981

They called 1968 the "Year of the Pitcher." Pitchers were never more dominant. Denny McLain won 31 games for the Detroit Tigers, becoming baseball's first 30-game winner since 1934. Don Drysdale of the Dodgers pitched six shutouts in a row to break a 64-year-old major league record.

One-fifth of all games played that year were shutouts. League batting averages nosedived. In the American League, the average sank to .230; in the National League, to .243. Not since 1908 had they been so low. The next season, 1969, rule makers lowered the pitching mound by five inches, one-third of its height, in an effort to restore the balance between pitchers and hitters.

In the "Year of the Pitcher," *the* pitcher in the National League was Bob Gibson of the St. Louis Cardinals, who won the first of his three Cy Young Awards that season. Gibson pitched 305 innings, winning 22 games, losing only 9. He had 13 shutouts; he had 268 strikeouts, tops in the league.

But Gibson's most stunning statistic that year was his 1.12 earned run average, the lowest in history for a 300-inning season. During one stretch, Gibson allowed only two runs across 92 innings.

Bob Gibson was a true power pitcher, with a fastball that would rise and explode. He also had a darting sinker, a good curve, and pinpoint control. Speed and control are a deadly combination. From 1963 through 1972, Gibson averaged slightly better than 19 wins per season. He struck out more than 200 batters nine times and led the league in shutouts four times. He tossed a no-hitter at the Pirates in 1971.

Gibson was also successful because he was such a fearsome figure on the mound. Tim McCarver, who caught Gibson, once told Roger Angell of the *New Yorker:* "There was no guile to his pitching, just him glaring down at the hitter."

Gibson himself would probably agree with that judgment. "If there's one thing I can't stand, it's to lose," he once said. "I don't even let my ten-year-old daughter beat me in ticktacktoe."

With that kind of drive, it's easy to understand Gibson's outstanding record in World Series play.

Few pitchers were as dominating on the mound as Bob Gibson. *(National Baseball Library)*

By 1961, Gibson had solved his control problems and began his remarkable career. He finished with 251 wins, the most by any pitcher in Cardinal history. He became the second pitcher in history to strike out 3,000 batters. (He ended with 3,117 strikeouts for his career).

Gibson also won nine consecutive Gold Gloves for his fielding excellence. And his hitting talents mustn't be overlooked. He had 24 career homers, plus 2 in World Series play.

Gibson achieved all that he did despite several serious injuries. They included a badly strained elbow in 1966, a broken leg the next season, and badly torn knee ligaments in 1973 that led to surgery.

But it wasn't pain or injury that caused Gibson to give up the game. Early in September 1975, Pete LaCock of the Cubs, a .220 hitter at that point, hammered a grand slam home run off one of Gibson's pitches. If he couldn't dominate hitters such as LaCock, Gibson decided, it was time to quit.

In the opening game of the 1968 Series, in which he beat Denny McLain and the Tigers, 4–0, Gibson set a Series record by striking out 17. He went on to strike out a total of 35 in that Series, which is also a record.

Gibson won 7 Series games during his career, which puts him second to Whitey Ford, who has 10. Two of his victories were the deciding games in 1964, when the Yankees were the opposition, and 1967, against the Red Sox.

Gibson, a sickly child who almost died, went on to star in both basketball and baseball in high school. After attending Creighton University on a basketball scholarship, Gibson agreed to sign with the Cards for a bonus of $4,000. Assigned to the club's Omaha (Nebraska) farm team, he was found to be fast but wild. Said a Cardinal official: "Gibson could throw the ball through the side of a barn—if he could only hit the barn."

Gibson on his way to victory in the seventh game of the 1964 World Series *(National Baseball Library)*

Don Drysdale

Born: July 23, 1936; Van Nuys, California
Height: 6′5″ Weight: 208
Threw right-handed, batted right-handed
Elected to the Hall of Fame in 1984

A tall right-hander, the Dodgers' Don Drysdale fired his 90-plus mile-an-hour fastball with such a big sidearm motion that it seemed to rocket in from third base. He combined that fearsome weapon with a deserved reputation as a knockdown artist to become one of the standout pitchers of the 1960s.

"I was the kind of guy," Drysdale once said, "who would hit his grandmother to win a game, and sing songs at a baseball writers' dinner the next night."

Knockdowns had more than merely strategic value to Drysdale. They were also used to settle scores. As he put it, "My own rule was two for one—if one of my teammates got knocked down, then I knocked down two guys on the other team."

Many hitters feared Drysdale. And they had reason to. He hit 154 batters during his career, the National League record.

Headhunters are a rare breed nowadays. That's because the game has changed. In Drysdale's time, pitchers were permitted to pitch inside to move back a batter crowding the plate. A pitcher might actually knock a batter down to make his message clear. Umpires don't allow such tactics today. A pitcher can be ejected on the spot if he hits a batter under circumstances that seem other than purely accidental.

Besides his reputation as an enforcer, Drysdale was also known for his temper. Once, after giving up a home run, he threw the ball into the stands. It "slipped," he claimed.

Drysdale's greatest personal achievement came in 1968, when he pitched six consecutive shutouts on his way to 58⅔ consecutive scoreless innings, the major league record. Just to complete six straight games is unheard of nowadays. It was still quite an accomplishment in Drysdale's day. To do it without giving up a run seems beyond belief. (Drysdale's record was broken by another Dodger, Orel Hershiser, in 1988. Hershiser pitched 59 consecutive scoreless innings.)

Drysdale joined the Dodgers in 1956, a year after Sandy Koufax. After Drysdale joined Sandy Koufax in the Dodger rotation, they often overpowered the opposition. Between 1963 and 1966, they pitched the team into the World Series three times. Unlike Koufax, however, Drysdale had some minor league seasoning, including a summer with Bakersfield (California) in the California League and the 1955 season at Montreal, an International League club at the time. Drysdale won 17 games for the Dodgers in their last year in Brooklyn. He pitched the team's first West Coast game in 1958, a loss to the Giants.

In the winter of 1965, following a season in which Drysdale and Koufax had a combined record of 49–20, the two staged a joint holdout. They sought a three-year, $1 million contract, the money to be divided evenly. They didn't get anywhere near what they asked for, but their holdout helped to pave the way for the huge amounts that superstars would be paid in the decades that followed. In hindsight, $1 million seems a bargain.

During his 14-year career, Drysdale compiled a 209–166 record, with a 2.95 earned run average. He led the National League in strikeouts three times. In 1962, when he posted a 25–9 record, he won the Cy Young Award.

Following his retirement as an active player in 1969, Drysdale remained in the spotlight. He appeared on many television shows as a guest star and became a broadcaster for the Angels and then the White Sox before settling down again with the Dodgers.

Drysdale was a Dodger, and only a Dodger, throughout his 13-year major league career. *(Wide World)*

In winter of 1965, Drysdale (right) and Sandy Koufax staged a joint holdout. *(Wide World)*

Whitey Ford

Born: October 21, 1928; New York, New York
Height: 5′10″ Weight: 181
Threw left-handed, batted left-handed
Elected to the Hall of Fame in 1974

"Cool. Crafty. Nerves of steel." Those are the words Yankee slugger Mickey Mantle used to describe his teammate and buddy Whitey Ford.

Said Mantle: "I don't care what the situation was, how high the stakes were—the bases could be loaded and the pennant riding on every pitch, it never bothered Whitey. He pitched his game."

There's plenty of evidence to support Mantle's judgment. A pitcher on no less than 11 league championship Yankee teams, Ford won more World Series games—10—than any other pitcher in baseball history. He also achieved the highest winning percentage—.690, based on 236 wins, 106 losses—of any pitcher with more than 200 victories.

As a teenager, Edward Charles Ford played high school and sandlot baseball in New York City's borough of Queens. He was scouted and signed by the Yankees for a $7,000 bonus in 1946. That amount enabled the club to outbid the Red Sox and Dodgers, both of whom were very interested in the young man.

After two full years and part of a third in the minor leagues, Ford was called up by the Yankees. It didn't take long for him to display his coolness under fire. In September 1950, manager Casey Stengel started Whitey in a crucial game against the Tigers. First-place Detroit led New York by half a game. Whitey responded by turning back the Tigers, 8–1. The victory boosted the Yankees into first place and helped send them on their way to the league title.

In the World Series against the Phillies, Stengel started Ford in the fourth, and what proved to be the deciding, game. "I never get butterflies," the cocky Ford told reporters before the game. He then went out and blanked the Phillies for eight innings and won, 5–2. He missed the shutout in the ninth when outfielder Gene Woodling dropped a fly ball.

Just as Whitey's career was getting launched, he was drafted into the army. The Korean War, in which members of the United Nations came to the aid of South Korea, was heating up. While Whitey never saw action in Korea, he lost the seasons of 1951 and 1952 to military service.

Once he returned to the Yankees, Whitey quickly regained his form. He had an 18–7 record in 1955, another pennant-winning season for the Yankees.

By 1956, Whitey was the ace of the Yankee staff. That season, with a 2.47 earned run average, he captured the first of his two ERA titles.

Despite Whitey's wizardry, Yankee manager Casey Stengel seldom used him in the regular starting rotation. He preferred to save him for use against the stronger teams and kept him on the bench when the team faced weak ones.

When Ralph Houk replaced Stengel as the Yankee skipper in 1961, he quickly changed that policy. To Houk, Whitey was the "Chairman of the Board."

Whitey responded to being used more often with a 25–4 record, his first 20-win season. (How many such seasons might he have had if used more regularly by Stengel?) The total included a streak of 14 consecutive victories. He won the Cy Young Award that year.

In the 1961 World Series, Ford won two games and topped Babe Ruth's string of 29⅔ scoreless innings. The record had stood for 43 years. Whitey extended the streak to 33⅔ innings in the World Series the following year, 1962, when he also won his record-setting tenth game.

After Ford retired as a player in 1967, he remained with the Yankees as a scout and pitching coach. He also served as the team's pitching coach in Florida each spring, an assignment he especially enjoyed.

Known as "Slick," Ford had an exceptional curveball and a "sneaky" fastball. It was very fast but it didn't appear to be. *(all photos National Baseball Library)*

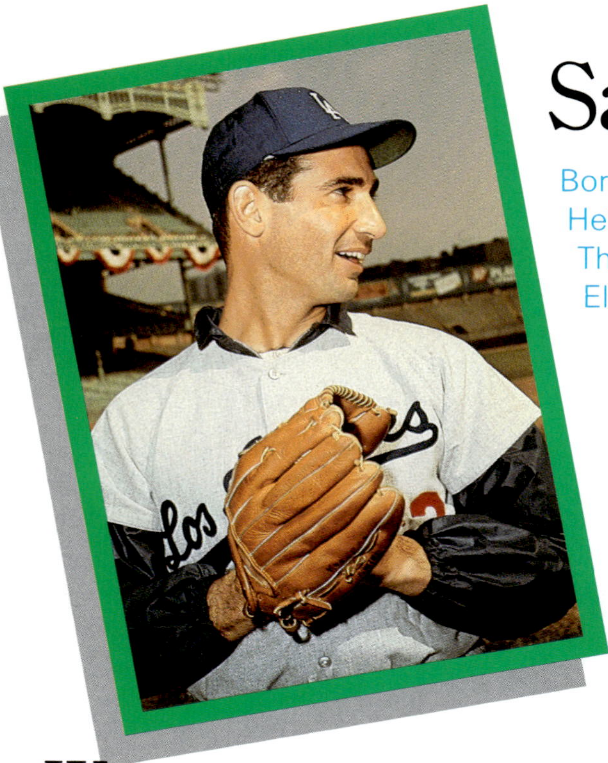

Sandy Koufax

Born: December 30, 1935; Brooklyn, New York
Height: 6′2″ Weight: 198
Threw left-handed, batted right-handed
Elected to the Hall of Fame in 1972

"When you had a game you absolutely had to win," said former Dodger pitcher Joe Black, "Koufax was untouchable." It's true. For five years, from 1962 through 1966, the Dodgers' Sandy Koufax and his dazzling fastball dominated baseball as perhaps no pitcher before or since. "Untouchable" was the word for him.

During those five seasons, Koufax won 111 games, lost only 34, and pitched four no-hitters, one of them a perfect game. He led the league in earned run average five times and in strikeouts four times. He won the Most Valuable Player Award in 1963 and Cy Young Awards in 1963, 1965, and 1966.

Born in Brooklyn in 1935, Sanford Koufax grew up in a home where sports were never discussed. His mother was an accountant. His stepfather was a lawyer. But Sandy became more involved with sports than with books, and although his ambition was to be an architect, he ended up going to the University of Cincinnati on a basketball scholarship.

Dodger scouts had known of Sandy's talents as a Brooklyn sandlot pitcher. In Cincinnati he played baseball as well as basketball, and when the young lefty began overwhelming college batters, the club offered him a $14,000 signing bonus. Sandy accepted the offer. When the 19-year-old Koufax joined the team in 1955, it included such all-time greats as Jackie Robinson, Roy Campanella, Duke Snider, and Pee Wee Reese.

At first, Sandy was not only very fast but very wild. Of his first three seasons with the club, 1957 was the best, when he posted a 5–4 record. That year the Dodgers stunned the baseball world with the news they were leaving Brooklyn for Los Angeles.

In Los Angeles, Koufax began to hit his stride. He earned headlines on August 31, 1959, by striking out 18 Cub batters, which tied a major league record at that time.

The promise of 1959 began to be fulfilled in 1961. Koufax won 18, lost 13, and led the National League with 269 strikeouts.

In 1962, Koufax and the Dodgers appeared to be on their way to the league title. But in June,

Koufax pitches against the Twins in the 1965 World Series. Shortly after, he announced he would retire. *(National Baseball Library)*

Koufax injured his index finger and was sidelined for most of the season. The Dodgers lost the pennant in a playoff with the Giants. But for Sandy's injury, no playoff would have been necessary.

Koufax was never better than in 1963. He won 25 games, lost only 5, and led the league with 306 strikeouts and a 1.88 earned run average. In the World Series against the Yankees, he struck out the first 5 batters he faced and 15 overall in winning the first game. He also won the deciding fourth game.

Koufax had another banner year in 1964. But by this time he was suffering from traumatic arthritis in his left elbow. After a game, the trainer would put his arm in a rubber sleeve and soak the elbow in a bucket of ice for as long as an hour. Still, the elbow would swell scarily the next day and the pain seldom stopped.

Nevertheless, Koufax in 1965 won 26 games and lost only 8. He struck out 382 batters, a National League record.

On September 9 that year, Koufax pitched a perfect game—no hits, no runs, no batter reaching first base. It was the fourth no-hitter of his career.

In 1966, Koufax was at the peak of his fame. He won 27 games and his third Cy Young Award. In November that year, he announced he planned to retire. The reason: He was afraid that continued use of his left arm would lead to permanent injury. The Dodgers hoped he would change his mind but he never did.

Koufax was elected to the Hall of Fame in 1972—at 36, the youngest man ever to join that select group.

Koufax has his swollen arm iced after a game against the Cardinals in 1964. *(Wide World)*

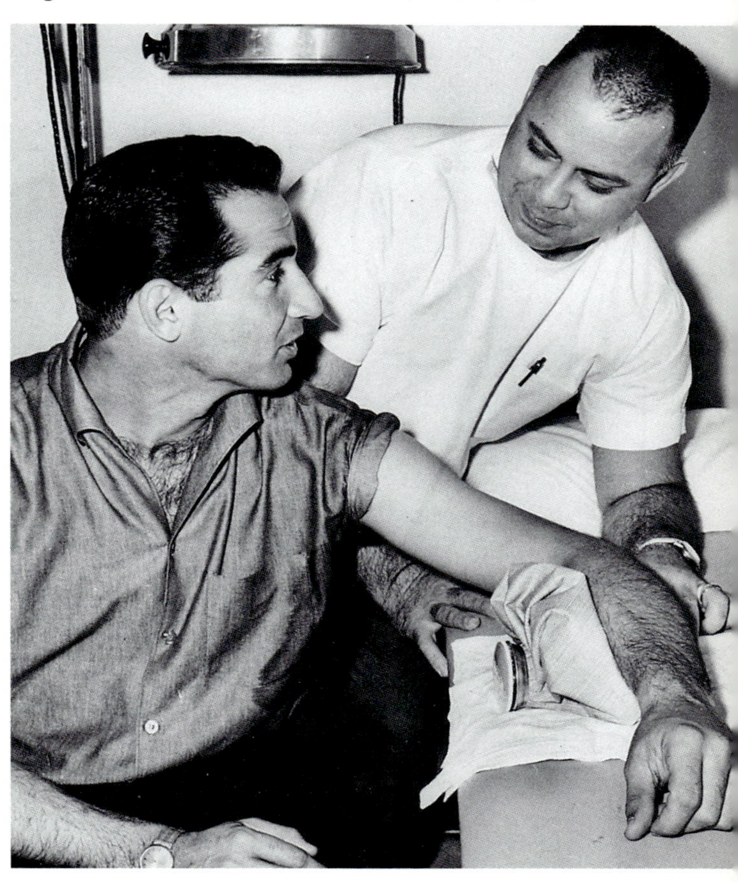

Robin Roberts

Born: September 30, 1926; Springfield, Illinois
Height: 6′1″ Weight: 200
Threw right-handed, batted right-handed and left-handed
Elected to the Hall of Fame in 1976

Robin Roberts became a pitcher almost by accident. As a kid, he was a third baseman, although he also played first base and the outfield once in a while. When he went to college at Michigan State and tried out for the baseball team, he was asked, "Well, where do you want to play?"

"What do you need?" Robin replied.

"Pitchers."

"Well, I'm a pitcher."

A 19-year career and 286 major league wins evolved from that answer.

Robin Roberts was the pride of the Philadelphia Phillies during the 1950s. For six consecutive seasons beginning in 1950 he won 20 or more games. In 1952, he won 28, the highest total in the National League in almost 20 years.

As a teenager, basketball was actually Robin's best sport. A 6-foot-1 forward, he received an offer of a basketball scholarship from Michigan State University. But then the baseball coach asked him that key question and turned him into a pitcher. He hurled two no-hitters for Michigan State, including one against the University of Michigan, the Spartans' archrival.

Several major league teams became interested in Robin, the Yankees, Red Sox, and Tigers among them. But the 22-year-old Roberts signed when the Phillies offered him a $25,000 bonus. A brief stay with Wilmington (Delaware) in the Inter-State League followed.

As a 22-year-old rookie in 1948, Roberts had a 7–9 record for the Phillies, who finished in sixth place. Both Roberts and the team improved in 1949, when Robin won 15 and lost 15.

Roberts had an unforgettable season in 1950. The Phillies were locked in a thrilling pennant race with the Brooklyn Dodgers. It came down to the final game of the season, played at Ebbets Field, Brooklyn's home park. In the tenth inning, Roberts led off with a single and scored on a home run off the bat of Dick Sisler. The 4–1 Philadelphia win, Robin's twentieth victory of the season, clinched the league championship for the Phils, the team's first pennant in 35 years.

In the World Series, the Phillies were overwhelmed by the Yankees, who won four straight. Robin never got another chance to appear in a World Series.

After the 1950 season, Roberts continued as one of baseball's brightest stars. He led the National League in victories every year from 1952 through 1955. He led the league in complete games, five times, from 1952 through 1956.

In 1952, Roberts looked like he might be the first National League pitcher to win 30 games since Dizzy Dean, who accomplished the feat in 1934. Roberts finished with a 28–7 record. There was no Cy Young Award in those years, but pitchers frequently won the Most Valuable Player Award—but Roberts did not. It went to Hank Sauer, a slugging outfielder for the Chicago Cubs, in what has often been looked upon as a puzzling choice.

Roberts was a workhorse with a capital W. For six consecutive seasons beginning in 1950 he pitched 300 or more innings. In 1953, he reached a high of 347 innings, with a league-leading 33 complete games. Pitchers of the 1990s do not even approach such numbers.

Throughout his long career, Roberts was also noted for his excellent control. He seldom walked a batter. But because his pitches were usually in or very close to the strike zone, he gave up an abundance of hits and home runs. Four times he led the league in home runs permitted, and his career total of 502 is a major league record.

When Roberts reached age 35, Philadelphia felt he was through and sold him to the Yankees, who, in turn, traded him to the Orioles. Roberts enjoyed several solid seasons with Baltimore, winning 42 games between 1962 and 1965.

After Baltimore released him, Roberts played briefly for Houston and Chicago in the National League. He won his last, and 286th, game for the Cubs in 1966. He wanted to continue pitching but an elbow injury put an end to his career.

Roberts was elected to the Hall of Fame in 1976.

Sold to the Yankees by the Phillies, Roberts pitches for the New York team at spring training in 1961. *(both photos National Baseball Library)*

Warren Spahn

Born: April 23, 1921; Buffalo, New York
Height: 6′ Weight: 183
Threw left-handed, batted left-handed
Elected to the Hall of Fame in 1973

Warren Spahn was the left-hander with the most wins of all time. His career won and lost record—363–245—is about the same as Sandy Koufax's and Don Drysdale's *combined.* And there are a good number of nine-man pitching staffs playing today whose victories, added together, do not even approach Spahn's career total.

Warren, who was named after Warren G. Harding, the 29th president, originally wanted to play first base. But in high school, when he was unable to beat out the team's first baseman, he switched to pitching.

Scouted and signed by the Boston Braves in 1940, Warren toiled for three years in the minor leagues. But World War II was under way, and just as he was ready to move to the major leagues, he was drafted into the army.

Warren served with the combat engineers in Europe, taking part in the bloody Battle of the Bulge and the desperate struggle by Allied forces to conquer central Germany. He earned three battle stars, a citation for bravery, and the Purple Heart for shell fragments in his foot.

It was 1946 when Spahn finally joined the Braves. The three years he spent in the army had postponed his first major league victory until he was 25 years old.

Spahn posted an 8–5 record in 1946, and the next year he was 21–10. It was the first of his 13 seasons as a 20-game winner. And with a 2.33 earned run average, he achieved the first of his three ERA titles.

In 1948, Spahn started slowly but was in peak form when the Braves launched a late-season drive for the pennant. Without much depth in his pitching staff, manager Billy Southworth relied on either Warren or Johnny Sain, who was to compile a 24–15 record, almost every day. "Spahn and Sain, and pray for rain," was a common saying among Boston fans.

The club edged out the St. Louis Cardinals for the title, but lost to the Indians in the World Series. Spahn, who was 15–12 for the season, lost the second game and won the fifth game in relief.

The years that followed were good ones for Spahn. He won the first of four consecutive strike-

Spahn and Johnny Sain (left) pitched the Braves to the pennant in 1948. *(Baseball Nostalgia)*

out titles in 1949. He won 21 games in both 1949 and 1950.

While Warren was thriving, the Boston club was not. In 1953, after years of declining attendance, the Braves moved to Milwaukee. The first year there, Warren won a career-high 23 games.

Spahn received the Cy Young Award in 1957, a banner year for both the Braves and himself. He won 21 games, lost only 11, and had a 2.69 ERA. The Braves won the pennant, then turned back the Yankees in the Series. The Braves repeated as pennant winners in 1958, but the vengeful Yankees captured the Series.

Spahn pitched two no-hitters in his career, one in 1960, the other in 1961, the year he turned 40.

When Spahn's won-lost record slipped to 18–14 in 1962 (hardly a slip one might say), some observers thought his retirement might be near. But Spahn didn't think so. He bounced back in 1963 to win 23, losing only 7.

The next season, although he had problems getting batters out, finishing with a 6–13 record, he still wouldn't quit. He thought he could become a winning pitcher again, and perhaps even top the National League record of 373 victories for a career.

Nineteen more wins were what he needed. Sold to the New York Mets, a last-place team at the time, baseball became a struggle for Spahn. He was 44 years old now and his breaking balls no longer dropped or danced. Batters knocked him out in the early innings.

"I can still pitch," he said in 1966 at the age of 45. But no one offered him a contract. Warren Spahn was the best pitcher of his day, but some of his fans wished he had given up the game a little earlier.

With 363 victories, Warren Spahn is the most successful lefty of all time. *(National Baseball Library)*

Satchel Paige

Born: July 7, 1906; Mobile, Alabama
Died: June 8, 1982
Height: 6′3″ Weight: 185
Threw right-handed, batted right-handed
Elected to the Hall of Fame in 1971

Asked to name the best pitcher he ever saw, Dizzy Dean said, "It's that old Satchel Paige." To Joe DiMaggio, Paige was "the best I ever faced, and the fastest."

He threw the ball overhand, sidearm, or submarine style, and he had a high kick like Dean's. He mowed down batters with a sizzling fastball, what he called his "bee ball," that appeared suddenly from behind that upraised foot.

"He was so fast, you couldn't bunt against him," said an opposing player. "It was nothing but fire."

Paige once estimated that he worked for 250 teams and participated in 2,500 games, winning some 2,000 of them. While statistics for the Negro leagues are incomplete and not easy to verify, no one doubts that Satchel Paige was one of the very best pitchers in baseball history, if not *the* best. He was also one of the longest lasting.

LeRoy Robert Page was born on July 7, 1906, in Mobile, Alabama, the seventh of 11 children. His father was a gardener, his mother a domestic worker. According to Satchel, the family added an *i* to the name, changing it to Paige, "to make it more high tone."

When LeRoy was only seven, his mother got him a job lugging satchels at a local train station. That's how he got his nickname. By the time he was 10, Satchel was pitching for his high school team. Later, when he started in semipro baseball, he was paid one dollar a game.

Paige signed his first professional contract in 1926, joining the Chattanooga Black Lookouts of the Negro Southern League. After a short stay with the Lookouts, he moved on to the Birmingham Black Barons and then the Nashville Elite Giants. Fans jammed ballparks, not only to see him pitch, but to watch him perform. He would warm up by fielding balls at third base, as well as clowning with players and spectators. Often he would promise to strike out the first nine batters, and then actually do it.

Well aware of his ability to draw crowds, Paige bounced from one team to another during the 1930s, selling his talents to the highest bidder. He was always on the move. He spent winters in the Caribbean and summers in the United States, pitching as many as 200 games a year and earning as much as $30,000 a season. At that time, the best major leaguers were earning about half that amount.

Paige joined the Kansas City Monarchs in 1938, and there he reached his greatest fame. He spent nine seasons with the Monarchs, pitching a few innings several times a week.

When Jackie Robinson signed to play for the Brooklyn Dodgers in 1947, he became the first African-American player to be accepted into the major leagues. Other black players were signed soon after, but not Paige. He knew his age was the reason—he was 40 years old at the time.

Finally, in July 1948, Bill Veeck, the owner of the Cleveland Indians, threw risk aside and signed Satchel on his forty-second birthday. Paige was the first African-American pitcher in the American League, the fifth black player in the majors.

Paige finished his rookie season with a 6–1 record and a 2.48 earned run average. In 1952, with the St. Louis Browns, he was the American League's number-one relief pitcher, boasting 10 saves and a 12–10 record.

After he retired as a major leaguer, Paige went back barnstorming, again drawing huge crowds wherever he appeared. As late as September 25, 1965, he emerged from retirement and pitched three scoreless innings for the Kansas City A's against the Red Sox. He was 59 years old at the time—the oldest man to appear in a major league game. Not until 1967, at the age of 61, did Paige quit baseball for good.

Paige joined the Kansas City Monarchs of the Negro American League in 1939 and remained with the team for nine seasons, pitching several times a week. *(Baseball Nostalgia)*

Paige tunes up for an appearance at New York's Yankee Stadium. *(National Baseball Library)*

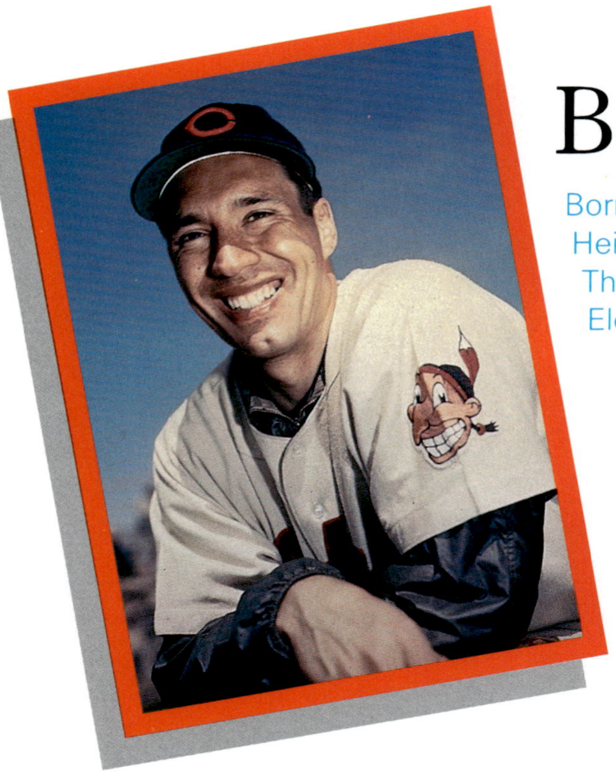

Bob Feller

Born: November 3, 1918; Van Meter, Iowa
Height: 6′ Weight: 185
Threw right-handed, batted right-handed
Elected to the Hall of Fame in 1962

An overnight sensation at the age of 17 and the game's dominant pitcher in the years before and after World War II, Bob Feller was also one of baseball's most electrifying players. Among his many achievements, including being the American League's strikeout champion seven times, were his three no-hitters and 12 one-hitters.

When Feller retired in 1956, the record book was crammed with his feats, achieved largely on the strength of his awesome fastball. Fans oohed and aahed just at the sight of him warming up.

Just how fast was Bob Feller? In 1945, owner Clark Griffith of the Washington Senators arranged to measure the velocity of Feller's fastball using photoelectric equipment he had installed over home plate in Griffith Stadium. Feller threw 30 or 40 pitches that night. One of them was clocked at 98.6 miles per hour as it crossed the plate. In an interview years later, Feller said, "I guess I was as fast as I ever was that night."

Robert William Andrew Feller was born and brought up on a corn and hog farm near Van Meter, Iowa. As a boy, he did the usual farm chores. Besides his chores and school, there wasn't much else except baseball. "I guess I could always throw hard," Feller once said, "even when I was eight or nine years old."

Bob played catch with his dad both summer and winter. When he was 12 he and his father fenced off a pasture and built a ball field on it. It included a diamond, an outfield fence, a scoreboard, and even a small grandstand. Feller's team of local farm boys played other teams from as far west as Omaha, Nebraska.

As a high school pitcher in 1934, Feller threw five no-hitters in the seven games he pitched. In his first start for the Farmers Union semipro team, he tossed a no-hitter, striking out 21. His second start was a one-hitter in which he fanned 23.

By the time Bob was 16, scouts were flocking to see him. In those days, baseball rules prevented major league teams from signing high school players. But the Cleveland Indians managed to sidestep the rules by signing the 16-year-old Feller and then assigning the contract to a minor league club. When the commissioner of baseball found out about the arrangement, he made the Indians pay the minor league team $7,500 to put things in balance.

During the break for the All-Star game in 1936, the St. Louis Cardinals traveled to Cleveland to play the Indians in an exhibition game. The Indians planned to use the contest to see what their 17-year-old sensation could do against major league talent. Inserted in the game in the fourth inning, Feller threw five warm-up pitches and then started blazing the ball past one astonished Cardinal after another. In the three innings he worked, Feller struck out eight. Home plate umpire Red Ormsby called Feller the fastest pitcher he had ever seen.

Feller joined the Indians in 1936 at the age of 17, then spent the next 20 years with the team. *(Baseball Nostalgia)*

During his rookie season, the 17-year-old Feller struck out 17 batters in a game against the Philadelphia A's. Here he cools off in the dressing room following that performance. *(Wide World)*

Afterward, a newspaper photographer asked Cardinal pitcher Dizzy Dean, baseball's number-one pitcher at the time, whether he would pose for a picture with Feller. Dean grinned and said, "You'd better ask *him* if he'll pose with *me.*"

After the game, Feller joined the Cleveland pitching staff. He made a handful of relief appearances before getting his first start in mid-August against the St. Louis Browns. Relying mainly on his fastball, but also on his good curve, Feller struck out 15 in his 4–1 victory. Three weeks later, in a game against the Philadelphia Athletics, Feller fanned 17 to set an American League record. And he still hadn't reached his eighteenth birthday.

The Indians' management handled the young man wisely, selecting his starting assignments carefully. In 1937, he pitched in 26 games, earning a 9–7 record. He had 150 strikeouts, an average of about one an inning. In 1938, appearing in 39 games, he enjoyed the first of five seasons with 240 or more strikeouts. He had his first 20-or-more-victory season in 1939, leading the league with 24.

Feller got off to an exceptional start in 1940, pitching a no-hitter on opening day, a feat not accomplished before or since. He won a career high of 27 games that season and lost only 11.

Feller works out before a game he pitched—and won—against the Red Sox early in the 1940 season. *(Wide World)*

World War II carved three full seasons and most of a fourth out of Feller's career. He entered the navy early in 1942 and ended up on the battleship *Alabama* in the South Pacific. The *Alabama*'s job was to protect American aircraft carriers, which were frequently attacked by Japanese torpedo bombers. Feller, who headed an antiaircraft-gun unit, saw plenty of action.

After Feller was discharged in 1945, he rejoined the Indians, and fans wondered whether his long absence from the game had eroded his skills. The results were a relief to everyone. In 1946, pitching 371 innings, Feller won 26 games and struck out 348. One of his victories was a no-hitter at Yankee Stadium.

It wasn't until 1948, his eighth full major league season, that the Indians won the league title and Feller got to pitch in the World Series, against the Boston Braves. In the opening game, Feller was matched against Johnny Sain in a scoreless pitching duel. In the eighth inning, Feller issued a base on balls. Phil Masi was sent in as a pinch runner, and the Braves sacrificed him to second.

All year long, the Indians had drilled on a clever pickoff play. On a prearranged signal, the pitcher would whirl and throw to second base, where shortstop Lou Boudreau would be waiting. When Masi took a long lead, the signal was flashed. Feller spun and fired. Boudreau gloved the ball and made the tag. But the umpire called Masi safe. Tommy Holmes singled later in the inning for the game's only run.

Newspaper photographs the next day seemed to indicate Masi was out. Feller has often described the game as his "toughest defeat."

Feller started the fifth game of the Series, but was driven out in the seventh inning, and the Braves won, 11–5. Cleveland eventually won the Series in six games. Feller's effort in game one was as close as he ever got to winning a World Series contest.

Feller's 22 wins in 1951 were the most for any

pitcher, but that was his last 20-victory season. In 1955, he was 4–4; in 1956, 0–4. He retired after the 1956 season. His uniform number, 19, was never again worn by a Cleveland player.

Bob Feller compiled a 266–162 lifetime record. How many games might he have won had it not been for those years of military service? Three hundred for sure. Four hundred? Perhaps. But even with those missing seasons, Bob Feller's 18-year career is studded with extraordinary achievements.

After he pitched a no-hitter against the Tigers in 1951, Feller held up three baseballs to indicate it was his third no-hitter. *(Wide World)*

The wind-up . . . and the delivery *(Wide World)*

Carl Hubbell

Born: June 22, 1903; Carthage, Missouri
Died: November 21, 1988
Height: 6′1″ Weight: 175
Threw left-handed, batted right-handed
Elected to the Hall of Fame in 1947

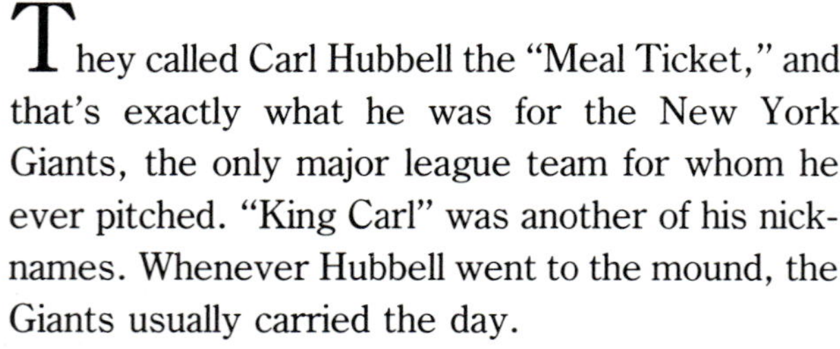

They called Carl Hubbell the "Meal Ticket," and that's exactly what he was for the New York Giants, the only major league team for whom he ever pitched. "King Carl" was another of his nicknames. Whenever Hubbell went to the mound, the Giants usually carried the day.

In 1933, with the Giants locked in a pennant race with the Pirates, Hubbell won 23 games, lost 12, posted a 1.66 earned run average, and was named the National League's Most Valuable Player. The Giants won the league championship and downed the Washington Senators in the World Series, where Hubbell won two games.

In 1936, Hubbell was the MVP again, winning a league-leading 26 games, as the Giants won another league pennant. They won yet again in 1937, behind Hubbell's 22 victories.

When he ended his career in 1943 at the age of 40, Hubbell had 253 lifetime victories, which stood as the National League record for a left-hander until broken by Warren Spahn years later.

Born in Missouri and brought up on an Oklahoma pecan farm, the tall, slim, and hungry-looking Hubbell was an impressive high school pitcher. He became even better during spring training with Oklahoma City of the Western League in 1925, when he began to throw a screwball.

Hubbell, being a left-hander, understood that left-handed hitters who faced him looked for a curve that would break away from them. But the screwball was a "reverse curve"; it shot in toward a lefty hitter.

To throw the screwball, or butterfly pitch, as it was also called, Hubbell had to twist his wrist to the right, in a clockwise direction. Doing so caused an unnatural pulling and jerking of the muscles in his lower arm.

Young Hubbell's Oklahoma City team sold his contract to the Detroit Tigers after the 1925 season. Detroit manager Ty Cobb told Hubbell not to throw the screwball. Cobb was afraid Hubbell would damage his valuable arm.

With no screwball, Hubbell struggled through two mediocre minor league seasons. By the fall of 1927, he was beginning to doubt whether he had a baseball future.

The Tigers gave up on Hubbell early in 1928 and released him. Carl then caught on with Beaumont in the Texas League, where he was permitted to use the screwball again. Immediately his prospects brightened. A scout for the New York Giants spotted him, and by midseason Carl was wearing a New York uniform. He appeared in 20 games for the Giants that season, winning 10 and finishing with a 2.83 earned run average.

The screwball, a nasty "reverse curve," was Hubbell's favorite pitch. *(Baseball Nostalgia)*

Hubbell pitched a no-hitter against the Pirates in 1929, and in 1933 he went 18 innings in a game against the Cards, winning, 1–0. That's equivalent to two complete games. He did not walk a single batter.

But Hubbell's greatest day in baseball came on July 10, 1934, when he was the starting pitcher for baseball's second All-Star game, played at New York's Polo Grounds.

Hubbell went to the mound to face an American League lineup that looked like this:

Charlie Gehringer, 2b
Heinie Manush, lf
Babe Ruth, rf
Lou Gehrig, 1b
Jimmie Foxx, 3b
Al Simmons, cf
Joe Cronin, ss
Bill Dickey, c
Lefty Gomez, p

Seldom has an All-Star lineup been so formidable. Virtually every player was a fearsome slugger. Every one of those players is today a member of baseball's Hall of Fame.

Leadoff hitter Gehringer opened the game with a single and then Manush walked. Catcher Gabby Hartnett went to the mound to speak to Hubbell. "Throw the screwball!" he said. "It always got *me* out."

Hubbell next faced Babe Ruth, and got Ruth to look at a called strike three. He struck out Lou Gehrig on four pitches. When Hubbell then fanned Jimmie Foxx, the crowd went wild.

Hubbell wasn't finished. To begin the second inning, he struck out Al Simmons and Joe Cronin. That made it five strikeouts in a row, and his victims were five of the best hitters in the game.

Hubbell left the game after three innings, with the National League ahead, 4–0. It's often forgotten that the American League rallied to earn a 9–7 victory. What hasn't been forgotten is Hubbell's performance that day, one of the most memorable in All-Star history.

Dizzy Dean

Born: January 16, 1911; Lucas, Arkansas
Died: July 17, 1974
Height: 6′3″ Weight: 202
Threw right-handed; batted right-handed
Elected to the Hall of Fame in 1953

Just rear back and let 'er go." That was Dizzy Dean's pitching philosophy. He once said, "Smart pitching, this so-called pitching to weaknesses of the hitters, is the bunk. You finally get so you're outsmarting yourself." Throughout his 10-year career with the St. Louis Cardinals and Chicago Cubs, Dean did what came naturally to him—kicked his leg high and threw hard.

With his scorching fastball, big curve, and breezy confidence, Dean led the National League in strikeouts for four consecutive seasons beginning in 1932. In 1934, the year he was named the National League's Most Valuable Player, he became only the fourth pitcher in modern baseball history to win 30 games.

Born in rural Arkansas in 1911, Jay Hanna Dean worked as a cotton picker as a child. He had almost no formal education, having quit school in second grade. "I didn't do too well in first grade, either," he once remarked. His zany behavior earned him his nickname.

At 16 he joined the army, but was discharged when the military found out how old he was. A St. Louis scout discovered him playing sandlot baseball in Texas. Soon Dean was pitching in the Texas League for Houston, a Cardinal farm team at the time. Dean won 26 games in 1931 and was promoted to the parent club the next year.

"I'll put more people in the park than anyone since Babe Ruth," the colorful Dean promised Branch Rickey, the Cardinal owner. And Dean delivered on his promise. Fans flocked to see him whenever he was scheduled to pitch.

In a Sunday game against the Cubs in 1933, Dean struck out 17, a league record at the time. He and his brother Paul, nicknamed Daffy, practically pitched the Cardinals to the league championship in 1934. Of the 95 games the Cardinal team won that year, the Dean brothers accounted for more than half of them—Dizzy, 30; Daffy, 19.

Detroit won the American League pennant that year. "Leave it to us," Dean told St. Louis fans before the first game of the World Series. "We'll make pussycats out of those Tigers." The Cardinals won the Series, but the Tigers didn't exactly roll over. It took seven games, with each of the Dean boys winning twice.

Dizzy had excellent seasons in 1935 and 1936. Then his career went downhill fast. Pitching in the 1937 All-Star game, Dizzy was struck in the left foot by a line drive off the bat of Cleveland outfielder Earl Averill. A broken toe was the result.

Doctors warned Dean not to try to pitch too soon, but he ignored the advice. When he resumed his place in the rotation, he strained his right shoulder while trying to favor the injured foot. Serious arm trouble followed. Before the season ended, the Cards dealt Dean to the Cubs.

Although he no longer had his speed or big curve, Dean still managed to win 16 games in three seasons with Chicago. After a token appearance with the St. Louis Browns in 1947, Dean retired to launch a successful career as a baseball broadcaster.

One other of Dean's achievements must be mentioned. In the seventh game of the 1934 World Series, Dean led off the inning with a double. His Cardinal teammates kept hitting and hitting. Dean came to bat a second time that inning and got a second hit. He ranks as the first and only pitcher to ever get two hits in one inning in the World Series.

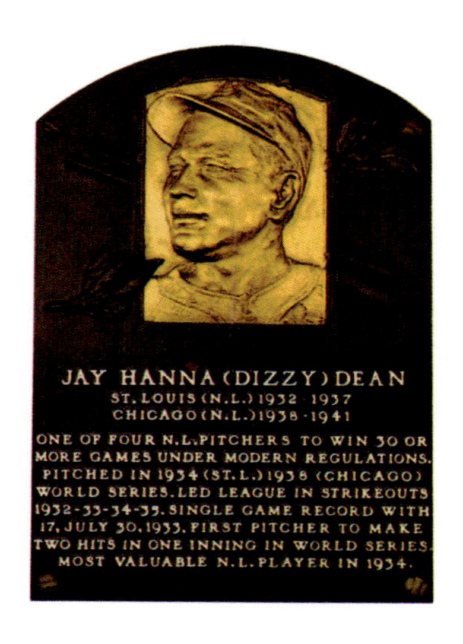

TOP: Dean greets Cardinal teammate Pepper Martin at the team's training camp in Bradenton, Florida, in 1933. *(Wide World)*

BOTTOM: Dean unlimbers at the Cardinals' Tampa, Florida, training camp in 1938. *(Wide World)*

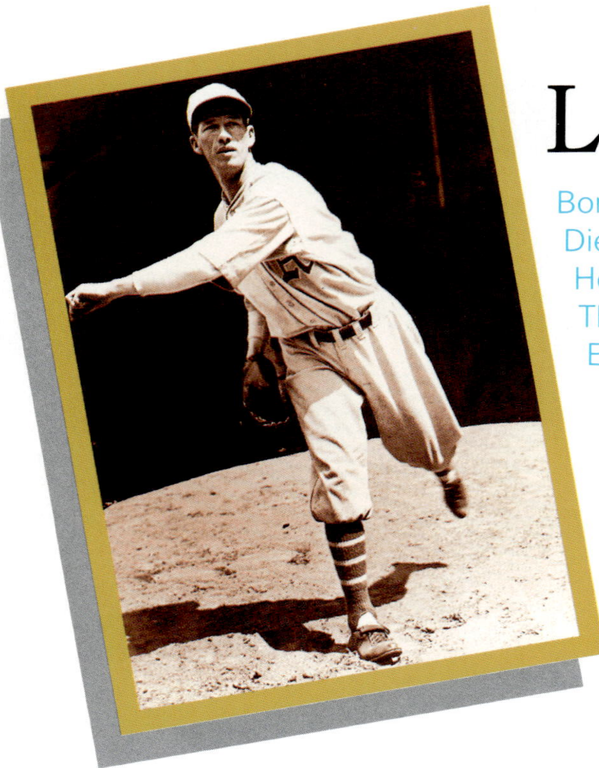

Lefty Grove

Born: March 6, 1900; Lonaconing, Maryland
Died: May 23, 1975
Height: 6′3″ Weight: 205
Threw left-handed, batted left-handed
Elected to the Hall of Fame in 1947

Bill James, whose yearly *Baseball Abstract* gives fresh insights into the game, calls Lefty Grove "the greatest pitcher of all time." James bases his judgment on the fact that Grove led the American League in earned run average nine times, and no other pitcher comes close to this achievement. Sandy Koufax, Walter Johnson, Christy Mathewson, and Grover Cleveland Alexander are next on the list, and they were ERA leaders only five times. To James, the ERA is the one best indicator of a pitcher's ability.

There is plenty of other evidence as to Grove's greatness. Although he didn't reach the majors until 1925, when he was 25, Grove still managed to win 300 games (while losing only 141) for the Philadelphia A's and Boston Red Sox. Five times he led the American League in winning percentage and seven times in strikeouts. Equally effective as a starter or reliever, Grove was named to four All-Star teams and voted the American League's Most Valuable Player in 1931.

The son of a coal miner, Robert Moses Grove, like his three brothers, went to work in the mines. In just one week, he learned to hate it.

In Midland, Maryland, where he started playing baseball for money, Grove played first base because there was no catcher in the area who could hold his flaming fastball. Once he was provided with a catcher, he quickly advanced from Midland to Martinsburg, West Virginia, to the Baltimore Orioles, a minor league club at the time.

In five seasons with Baltimore, Grove won 109 games and became a star. While with the Orioles, he earned as much as $7,500 a year, as much as the best major leaguers were receiving. The Philadelphia A's paid $100,600 for his contract, an almost unheard-of sum by standards of the day.

Grove was a high-kicking fastballer when he arrived in the American League. Because he was a little bit wild, more than a few batters were afraid to face him. As early as 1926, he began working on a curveball, and before long he had another effective weapon.

During 1931, Lefty was almost perfect. He won

Grove was very stingy with runs. Nine times he was the American League's ERA leader. *(Baseball Nostalgia)*

31 games and lost only 4, for a stunning .886 percentage. He hated to lose. At one stage during 1931, he was going for a record seventeenth straight victory. He lost, 1–0, because a young substitute left fielder misjudged a fly ball.

After the game, Lefty went berserk, practically wrecking the clubhouse. He tore steel lockers off the wall and ripped up his uniform. He threw anything he could get his hands on—bats, balls, shoes, gloves, and water buckets.

More than 40 years later, Lefty was interviewed about the game. "It still gets me mad when I think about it," he said.

Philadelphia traded Lefty to Boston after the season of 1933. His blazing speed was gone, but he developed a change of pace and a forkball to go with his curve. He still managed to be a winning pitcher one season after another. After winning victory number 300 in 1941, he decided it was time to call it quits.

While Lefty was always a fierce competitor, off the field he was calm and easygoing. Pitchers are often awarded "game balls" after wins. Lefty gave all 300 of his to kids' leagues.

Although he didn't become a major leaguer until he was 25, Grove still managed to win 300 games. *(National Baseball Library)*

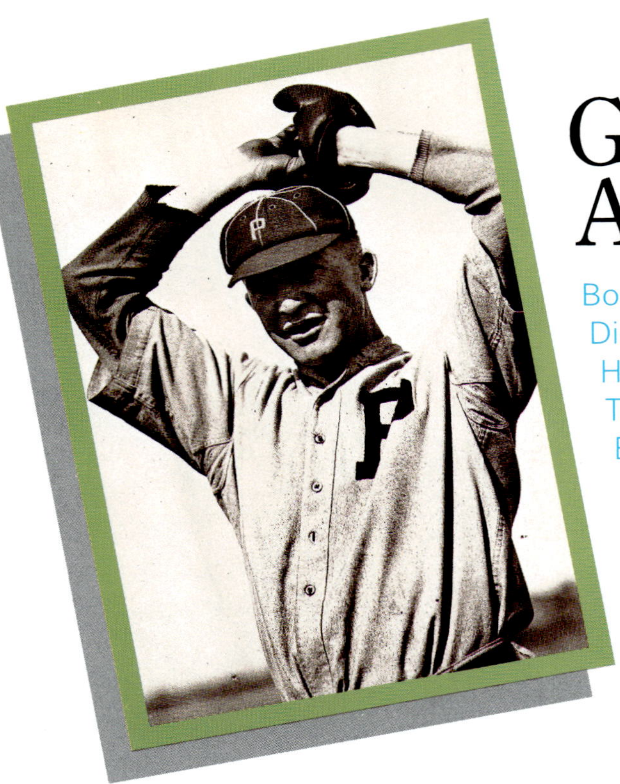

Grover Cleveland Alexander

Born: February 26, 1887; Elba, Nebraska
Died: November 4, 1950
Height: 6′1″ Weight: 185
Threw right-handed, batted right-handed
Elected to the Hall of Fame in 1938

They called him "Alexander the Great" during his years with the Philadelphia Phillies, and for good reason. Over seven seasons beginning in 1911, he won 190 games, and in three of those seasons he won 30 or more—31 in 1915, 33 in 1916, and 30 in 1917. His earned run average of 1.22 in 1915 stood as the National League record until 1968, when Bob Gibson of the St. Louis Cardinals had an ERA of 1.12.

Alexander ended his career in 1930 with 373 victories, which puts him in a tie with Christy Mathewson for third place on the all-time victory list. Alexander's 90 career shutouts are second only to Walter Johnson's total of 100. Of course, Alexander, for the most part, pitched during a period when batting averages were low and home runs scarcely existed.

But Alexander's glittering career brought him little peace or happiness. He suffered from epilepsy, a disorder of the nervous system. He also had a lifelong problem with alcohol.

Born on a farm in Elba, Nebraska, in 1887, one of 13 children, 12 of them boys, he was named after Grover Cleveland, the president of the United States at the time he was born. Tall, lanky, and freckle-faced as a boy, he hunted game birds with rocks, showing the throwing accuracy for which he would later become famous.

After several years in the semipro ranks, Grover, or Pete, as he was known, played minor league baseball with the Galesburg (Illinois) club in the Illinois-Missouri League and Syracuse (New York) in the New York State League. By the time he arrived in the major leagues with the Philadelphia Phillies in 1911, he was 24 years old.

Pete had a spectacular rookie season with the Philadelphia team. He led the National League with 28 wins, including seven shutouts.

His best pitch was a sinking fastball. He also boasted a fearsome curve. It broke less than most, but unusual for a curveball, was thrown with such velocity that it often left batters standing helplessly at the plate.

In 1915, with his 31 victories, Alexander led the Phillies to their first league championship. In the opening game of the World Series against Boston,

Alexander scattered eight hits, winning, 3–1. The Phillies then lost the next four games.

Philadelphia traded Alexander to Chicago in 1917. World War I was raging at the time. Alexander was called into the army and sent to France. An infantryman, he came under enemy fire and lost the hearing in one ear as a result of shells that exploded near him. He also showed the first signs of epilepsy.

When the war ended in 1918, Alexander returned to the Cubs. He had another fine year in 1920, compiling a 27–14 record. His earned run average of 1.91 was the best in the league and represented his fifth ERA title.

But 1920 was the last of Alexander's years of greatness. It was well known he was drinking too much. While his career continued for another decade, and he was to have a number of successful seasons, he never led the league in any category again. After the season of 1925, he entered a treatment center in an effort to bring his alcohol problem under control.

Long before he became president, Ronald Reagan starred in a film biography of "Alex the Great." *(Collection of Herman Darvick)*

Alexander's best pitch was a sinking fastball, but he also featured a fearsome curve. *(National Baseball Library)*

The Cubs sent Alexander to the St. Louis Cardinals in 1926. In the seventh game of the World Series that year, the Cardinals were leading, 3–2, in the seventh inning. The Yankees loaded the bases with two outs. St. Louis manager Rogers Hornsby brought the 39-year-old Alexander in from the bullpen to face Yankee rookie Tony Lazzeri. Alexander proceeded to strike out Lazzeri and set down the Yankees in the eighth and ninth innings. The Cards had won the Series, and Alexander was the hero.

But Alexander continued to drink heavily and he spent part of 1929 in a treatment center. In 1930, he pitched for Dallas in the Texas League, where he ended his career. The remainder of his life was often sad. He died in a rented room in St. Paul, Minnesota, at the age of 63.

Walter Johnson

Born: November 6, 1887; Humboldt, Kansas
Died: December 10, 1946
Height: 6′1″ Weight: 200
Threw right-handed, batted right-handed
Elected to the Hall of Fame in 1936

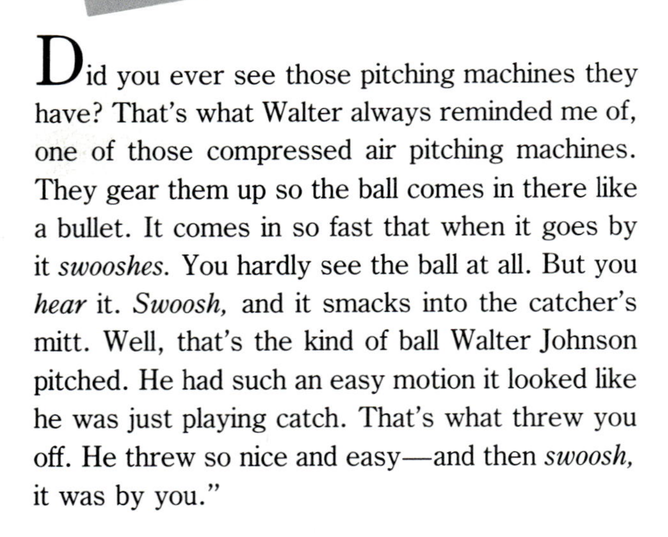

Did you ever see those pitching machines they have? That's what Walter always reminded me of, one of those compressed air pitching machines. They gear them up so the ball comes in there like a bullet. It comes in so fast that when it goes by it *swooshes*. You hardly see the ball at all. But you *hear* it. *Swoosh,* and it smacks into the catcher's mitt. Well, that's the kind of ball Walter Johnson pitched. He had such an easy motion it looked like he was just playing catch. That's what threw you off. He threw so nice and easy—and then *swoosh,* it was by you."

That's how Sam Crawford, a Hall of Fame outfielder for the Detroit Tigers, described Walter Johnson (in an interview with Lawrence S. Ritter, author of *The Glory of Their Times*). Many experts consider Johnson to be the hardest-throwing pitcher of his time. When he retired in 1927 after 21 seasons with the Washington Senators, his name dominated baseball's record book.

Walter Johnson won 416 games during his career, of which 110 were shutouts. Only Cy Young, with 511 wins, tops Johnson in career victories. No one has more shutouts. He shut out the Yankees three times in four days in 1908.

Johnson led the American League in strikeouts 12 times. He fanned a total of 3,508 batters during his career, a record that stood for half a century, but has been bettered in recent years by Nolan Ryan, Steve Carlton, and several other pitchers. In one season, 36 of Johnson's 37 starts were complete games. Today, with power pitchers in command, that kind of record is unthinkable.

What is startling about Johnson's career is that he was able to win so many games for such a pathetic team. During his 21 years with the Senators, they managed to win the American League pennant only twice. Usually they could be found at or very near the bottom of the league standings.

Time after time, mistakes by his teammates cost him a victory. But Johnson, who always seemed to see the bright side, never complained. In one game, Clyde Milan, a good outfielder, dropped a ball in the eleventh inning that resulted in Johnson

Johnson joined the Washington Senators about a year before this photograph was taken in 1908. *(National Baseball Library)*

Walter joined the Washington team in August 1907. He immediately impressed everyone with his speed and control. Sportswriter Grantland Rice nicknamed him "The Big Train," a reference to the speed and power of his fastball.

Johnson also made an impression with his mild manner. Most baseball players of the time were

losing, 1–0. In the dressing room after, Johnson was asked why he wasn't angry. "You know," he said, "Clyde doesn't do that very often."

Walter Perry Johnson was the son of a farmer who had traveled to Kansas by wagon from Ohio. After Walter was born in 1887, the family moved on to Olinda, California. Walter first pitched for Fullerton Union High School in Fullerton.

Later, at Weiser, Idaho, Walter played semipro baseball for the Weiser Telephone Company. The contract he signed provided him with $75 a month to pitch and dig holes for telephone poles.

When the Washington Senators heard incredible stories about Johnson's pitching, the club sent Cliff Blankenship, a catcher who was sidelined with an injury, to Idaho to take a look at him. When Blankenship saw Walter fire his fastball, he quickly got him to sign with the Senators.

Johnson won 416 games during his career; only Cy Young won more. *(both photos National Baseball Library)*

rough-hewn. They played poker, chewed tobacco, and hung out at saloons. Walter played checkers and went to the movies.

In 1910, Johnson was named to pitch opening day for the Senators at Nationals Park, then their home grounds. Before the game, President William Howard Taft threw out the first ball. It marked the first time the nation's chief executive had taken part in the "first ball" ceremony. A onetime catcher, President Taft watched as Johnson tossed a neat one-hitter to defeat the Philadelphia Athletics, 3–0.

It was Johnson who had caught the president's ceremonial first pitch. The day after the game, Johnson had a messenger bring the ball to the White House with a request for an autograph. Not only did the president sign the ball, but he wrote the following inscription:

To Walter Johnson, with the hope
he may continue to be as formidable
as in yesterday's game.

WILLIAM H. TAFT

The tradition of the president throwing out the ceremonial first ball lasted for as long as Washington had a major league team. (The team moved from Washington to Minnesota in 1961.) For years, Johnson was associated with the ceremony. Fourteen times, in fact, he was the opening day pitcher (winning nine times, with seven shutouts).

The 1910 season marked the first of 10 consecutive seasons in which Johnson won 20 or more games. He won 36 games in 1913, his highest total. No pitcher since has exceeded that figure. Johnson was virtually unbeatable that year. Besides the 36 wins (against only 7 losses, an .837 percentage), he led the league in strikeouts with 243. He pitched 11 shutouts and at one stage had 56 consecutive shutout innings.

Nineteen thirteen was the first year in which earned run averages were announced. Johnson's was 1.14. No one in either league did better than that until 1968, when Bob Gibson of the Cards posted an ERA of 1.12. Johnson won his first Most Valuable Player Award that year. He won the MVP prize again in 1924, when he was 36.

The Senators finally captured a league championship that season. Johnson's win over the New York Giants in the seventh game of the Series brought the team its first and only world title.

At the start of his twenty-first season, in 1927, Johnson was pitching batting practice at Washington's training camp in Tampa, Florida, when a line drive off the bat of Joe Judge struck him in the leg, and he went down. X rays showed the leg to be broken. Johnson was never a really effective pitcher after that. When the season was over, he decided to retire.

Johnson tried managing for a time, first with the Senators from 1929 to 1932, then with the Indians from 1933 to 1935. He was considered to be a much better pitcher than a manager.

Johnson retired to a farm he owned in Germanton, Maryland, not far from Washington. In 1936, along with Ty Cobb, Honus Wagner, Babe Ruth, and Christy Mathewson, Walter Johnson was one of the first group of players to be elected to the Hall of Fame.

When his career ended, Johnson retired to a farm in Germanton, Maryland. This high school was later named in his honor. *(Walter Johnson High School)*

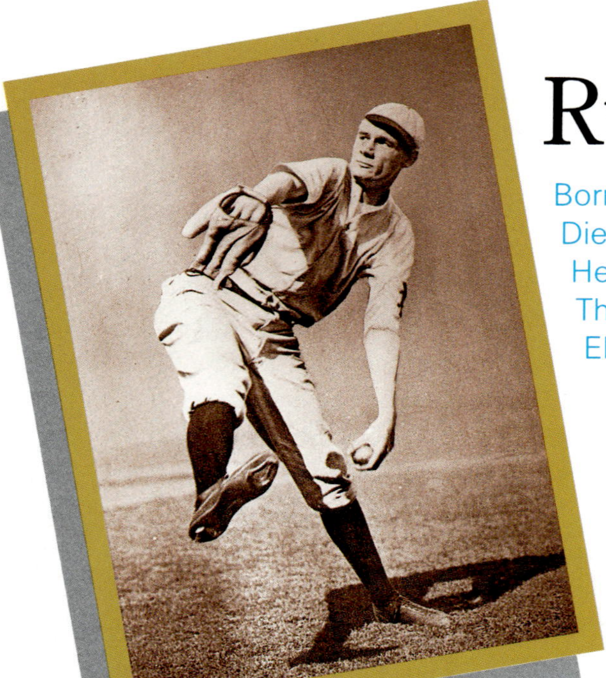

Rube Marquard

Born: October 9, 1889; Cleveland, Ohio
Died: June 1, 1980
Height: 6′3″ Weight: 180
Threw left-handed, batted right-handed and left-handed
Elected to the Hall of Fame in 1971

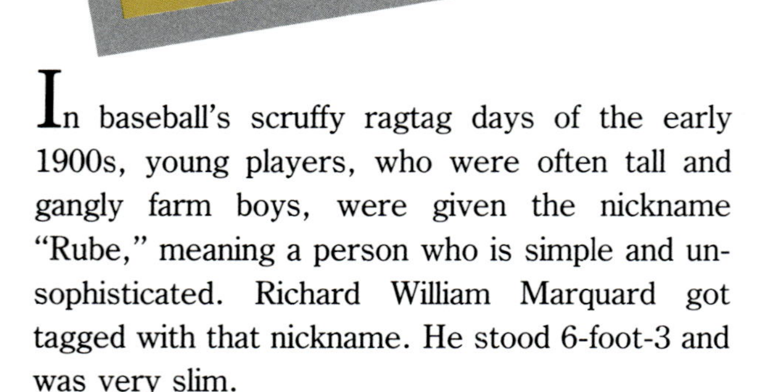

In baseball's scruffy ragtag days of the early 1900s, young players, who were often tall and gangly farm boys, were given the nickname "Rube," meaning a person who is simple and unsophisticated. Richard William Marquard got tagged with that nickname. He stood 6-foot-3 and was very slim.

But this Rube was no hick. His father was the chief engineer for the city of Cleveland, where the family of four boys and a girl lived.

When Richard was a young boy and began to show more than an average amount of interest in baseball, it upset his father, who looked upon the sport as a foolish pastime. Early in 1906, when Richard was 16, he was offered a tryout with the Waterloo team in the Ohio State League. His father told him that if he left home to play baseball not to come back. Richard went, anyway, riding freight trains and hitching rides to reach the team.

A day after he arrived in Waterloo, he pitched and won his first professional game. But after the Waterloo manager refused to offer him a contract, the homesick Marquard returned to Cleveland and sought his father's forgiveness.

Back home, Marquard worked for an ice cream company, earning $25 a week. He pitched for the company's baseball team. After scouts spotted his talent, Marquard signed a $200-a-month contract with Indianapolis of the American Association in 1906. Optioned to Canton (Ohio) for a year, Marquard returned to Indianapolis in 1908 and had a brilliant season, winning 28 games and leading the league in strikeouts.

A sportswriter for the *Indianapolis Star* compared Richard to another left-hander, the famous Rube Waddell. That's when people started calling him Rube. But about the only thing that Marquard had in common with Waddell was that they both pitched left-handed.

After Marquard's spectacular 1908 season in Indianapolis, major league teams launched a bidding war for his services. Marquard agreed to an $11,000 offer from the New York Giants, a record amount at the time.

Marquard struggled for a couple of seasons after joining the Giants, and sportswriters began calling him the "$11,000 lemon." But Giant coach Wilbert Robinson worked with the young man, helping him to improve his curve and perfect his delivery.

By 1911, the Giants' investment in Marquard began paying dividends. Rube had a 24–7 record, the first of three consecutive seasons in which he had 20 or more wins. In each of those three years, the Giants won the National League pennant.

In 1912, when Marquard won a league-leading 26 games, he set a major league record that still stands by winning 19 games in a row. As he liked to point out, the record would have been 20 under later rules, for he entered one game as a reliever with the Giants trailing, 5–2, and the team rallied to win. But under the rules then in effect, the victory went to the starting pitcher.

When Marquard started having problems with Giant manager John McGraw, he engineered a trade to Brooklyn. He helped the team, then known as the Robins, with two league championships. Marquard spent his last four major league seasons with the Boston Braves. He finished his career with 201 victories.

Rube found it difficult to give up baseball, his great love. He pitched for several minor league teams during the mid- to late 1920s, served as an umpire for the Eastern League in 1931, became a coach and a scout for Atlanta in the Southern League in 1932, and closed out his career by managing Wichita in the Western League in 1933.

Marquard won 19 straight games in 1912, holding the opposition to only 49 runs. *(National Baseball Library)*

Chief Bender

Born: May 5, 1884; Brainerd, Minnesota
Died: May 22, 1954
Height: 6′2″ Weight: 185
Threw right-handed, batted right-handed
Elected to the Hall of Fame in 1953

Connie Mack, who was manager of the Philadelphia Athletics for no fewer than 50 years and who probably witnessed more baseball games than any person who ever lived (he died in 1955), was once asked to recall some of the game's great pitchers. "If I had all the men I ever handled and they were in their prime," said Mack, "and there was one game I wanted to win above all others, Albert would be my man. He was my greatest 'money' pitcher."

Albert was Charles Albert Bender, known to everyone as "Chief." One of 13 children born to a Chippewa mother on the White Earth Indian Reservation in Brainerd, Minnesota, in 1884, he left home at the age of seven to attend the Carlisle Indian School at Carlisle, Pennsylvania. In time, he became one of the school's finest athletes, starring in both baseball and football.

After graduating from Carlisle in 1902, Bender played semipro baseball for a Harrisburg, Pennsylvania, club. Occasionally the team would schedule exhibition games against major leaguers. One day the 18-year-old Bender got the opportunity to pitch against the Chicago Cubs, and beat them. When news of the victory reached Philadelphia and Connie Mack, who besides managing the team also owned it, he promptly signed "the Chief" to a contract that paid him $300 a month.

The Chief was an instant success. Early in the 1903 season, Mack used Bender in a relief role against Boston. Bender, despite the lack of any minor league experience, hurled six innings and earned the victory, the first of 210 major league games he was to win.

The Chief enjoyed five championship seasons with the A's. In the 1905 World Series, he shut out the New York Giants for Philadelphia's only win. He tossed a three-hitter against Chicago in the 1910 Series to win, 4–1. The following year, he won two of three Series decisions against the Giants. He also won two games in the 1913 Series, including the first game. He thus became the first pitcher in baseball history to win six World Series games.

The Chief had an excellent fastball and a sharp-breaking overhand curve. Each pitch he delivered with a high leg kick. The spitball and other trick pitches were legal in those days. The Chief's specialty was the "talcum powder ball." Before each delivery, he would rub one side of the ball against a small bag of powdery talc he kept in his pocket. The talc would make that side of the ball as smooth as glass, which caused it to drop sharply as it neared the plate.

Of all his games with the Athletics, Bender's greatest was perhaps a 4–0 no-hitter he hurled against Cleveland in 1910. Only a walk prevented it from being a perfect game.

The Chief had many interests outside of baseball. He played golf, painted, and gardened. He was skilled at billiards and trap shooting, and was an expert on diamonds and other precious gems.

Once his career as a pitcher came to an end, Bender began a long tour of duty as a manager, coach, and scout. It included five years as coach at the U.S. Naval Academy at Annapolis, Maryland.

Chief Bender returned to the A's as a scout in 1945 and was a coach for the team in 1953, the year he was elected to the Hall of Fame. His remarkable baseball career spanned more than half a century.

ABOVE: Bender's name was Charles, but everyone called him "Chief." *(National Baseball Library)*

LEFT: Bender, winding up to fire one across the plate *(National Baseball Library)*

Christy Mathewson

Born: August 12, 1880; Factoryville, Pennsylvania
Died: October 7, 1925
Height: 6′1½″ Weight: 195
Threw right-handed, batted right-handed
Elected to the Hall of Fame in 1936

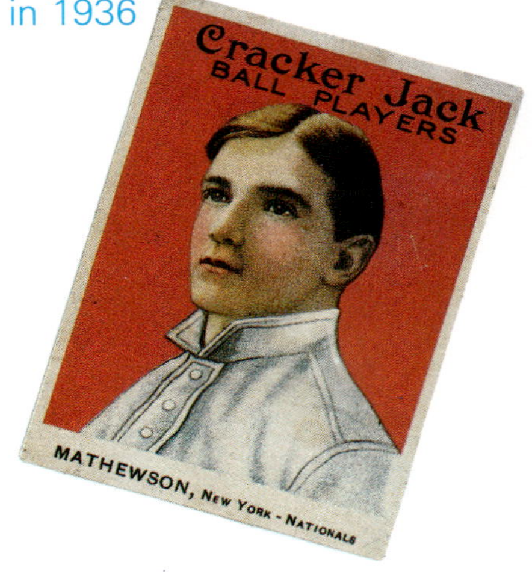

Tall, blond, and good-looking, Christy Mathewson was baseball's first real hero. He had brains and skill, courage and stamina. It was said he did not drink or smoke (although he did occasionally), and in a day when a college education was something of a rarity, Mathewson had attended Bucknell University in Lewisburg, Pennsylvania. Parents pointed to him as a model for their sons.

As a pitcher with the New York Giants, Mathewson had few equals. During a 12-year span beginning in 1903, Mathewson never won fewer than 22 games, and four times he won 30 or more. His lifetime record of 373 wins has been equaled or surpassed by only three other pitchers.

Christopher Mathewson was born on August 12, 1880, in Factoryville, Pennsylvania, the oldest of five children. He attended Keystone Academy and, later, at Bucknell, starred in football and basketball as well as baseball. He was also class president.

Christy left Bucknell in 1899 to sign with Taunton (Massachusetts) in the New England League. The following year, after he had won 20 games for Norfolk in the Virginia League, the Giants paid $2,000 for his contract.

At the time, the Giants were one of the saddest teams in the National League. They finished next to last in 1901, Mathewson's rookie season. But by 1904, when Matty won 33 games, the team had become the league's best.

Mathewson starred in the 1905 World Series, in which the Giants, wearing black uniforms with white belts, played the Philadelphia Athletics. It was called the "shutout Series," because in each of the five games played the losing team failed to score.

In the first game, Mathewson tossed a four-hitter, stopping the A's, 3–0. Game two saw the A's even matters behind Chief Bender. A rainout in Philadelphia enabled Mathewson to start the third game, and he pitched another four-hitter, winning, 9–0. Joe McGinnity won the fourth game for the Giants, and then Mathewson wrapped up the Series with a six-hitter, winning, 2–0. In his three shutouts, Mathewson allowed only 14 hits.

Although the Giants did not win another league championship until 1911, Mathewson continued to have one outstanding year after another. He won 37 games in 1908, a National League record for the 1900s that still stands. He appeared in 56 games that season, pitched 391 innings, and hurled 12 shutouts. He lost only 11, for a .771 percentage.

In four World Series, Mathewson's combined earned run average was a brilliant 1.15. He won five Series games, and lost five.

Mathewson mowed down hitters with a good fastball, a sweeping curve, and his fabulous fadeaway, what has been described as a "reverse curve," a pitch that behaved much like Carl Hubbell's screwball, but broke in toward a right-handed batter. The fadeaway was effective because Mathewson delivered it with the same overhead motion he used with his other pitches.

Mathewson's last standout year was 1914, when he finished with 24 victories. His twelfth season of 20-plus wins, it brought his lifetime victory total to 361. When he retired in 1916, the total stood at 373.

In all of baseball history, only Cy Young had done better. Young won 511 games. In the years that followed his retirement, Mathewson's total was equaled by Grover Cleveland Alexander and topped by Walter Johnson.

Mathewson served as manager of the Cincinnati Reds after his playing career ended. He also coached for the Giants for a time. In 1919, Mathewson was found to have tuberculosis, an infectious disease of the lungs. The disease took his life at the age of 45 in 1925.

Tall and good-looking, with brains and skill, Christy Mathewson was the Tom Seaver of his day. *(National Baseball Library)*

Three Finger Brown

Born: October 19, 1876; Nyesville, Indiana
Died: February 14, 1948
Height: 5′10″ Weight: 175
Threw right-handed, batted right-handed
Elected to the Hall of Fame in 1949

When he was born in 1876, the centennial year of America's independence, his parents named him Mordecai Peter Centennial Brown. But in baseball he was always known as "Three Finger" Brown because he had badly mangled two fingers of his pitching hand in a childhood accident.

As a seven-year-old farm boy, Brown was playing in the fields near his home when he got his right hand caught in a feed cutter being operated by his brother. Doctors had to amputate the index finger of his right hand just above the first knuckle. The little finger was rendered useless in the accident.

Oddly, the mutilated right hand helped to make Brown one of the most effective pitchers of his day. He gripped and released the ball in such a way that the spin was imparted mainly by the thumb. The result was one of the meanest curveballs in baseball history. It broke down and away from a right-handed hitter, and down and into a left-hander. Both were frustrated by it. When a batter did manage to get his bat on the pitch, he almost always hit it on the ground.

Brown himself was quick to admit that his gnarled hand worked to his advantage. "It gives me a bigger dip," he said.

Brown was a success from the beginning. At Terre Haute (Indiana) in the Three-I League in 1901, he won a league-leading 23 games. (The three *I*'s were the states of Indiana, Illinois, and Iowa.) He got to like the city so much, he made it his lifelong home.

In 1902, with Omaha of the Western League, Brown did even better, winning 27 times. The National League's St. Louis Cardinals then purchased his contract. After a rookie season in which the won 9 and lost 13, the Cards traded him to the Chicago Cubs.

That was in 1904. Brown pitched for the Cubs for nine seasons and won 20 or more games in six of them. Four times—in 1906, 1907, 1908, and 1910—he helped Chicago to win the National League championship. Brown, who was to win 239 games during his career, compiled a 5–4 record in World Series competition.

Brown won 26 of 32 decisions for the 1906 Cubs,

often described as one of the best teams in baseball history. The team won a record 116 games, lost only 36, and left the second-place New York Giants 20 games behind. The 1906 Cubs featured the famous Tinker-to-Evers-to-Chance double-play combination. They also had a hard-hitting trio of outfielders, and a superb pitching staff headed by Brown. No team before or since has won 116 games in a season.

Some of Brown's most memorable games were pitched against Christy Mathewson of the New York Giants. The two faced each other 24 times; Brown won 13 of the contests.

After almost a decade in Chicago, Brown was traded to Cincinnati. He spent one season with the Reds before switching to the St. Louis club of the Federal League, an upstart major league. He was back with the Cubs in 1916, but won only two games before drifting to the minor leagues. He played at Columbus, Indianapolis, and Terre Haute (Indiana) where he ended his career in 1920.

Brown admitted his maimed right hand was a big advantage in getting his curveball to break sharply. *(National Baseball Library)*

Cy Young

Born: March 29, 1867; Gilmore, Ohio
Died: November 4, 1955
Height: 6′2″ Weight: 210
Threw right-handed, batted right-handed
Elected to the Hall of Fame in 1937

Cy Young won 511 major league games, more than any pitcher in baseball history. It's one of those records that most experts consider to be unbreakable. Walter Johnson, who is second to Young in career wins, had "only" 416. Young also pitched three no-hitters and, on May 5, 1904, a perfect game.

In 1956, to honor this great pitcher, Ford Frick, then the commissioner of baseball, announced an award to be given to the most valuable pitcher each year in Cy's name. One award was presented from 1956 through 1966; two, one in each league, have been awarded since 1967. Today, the Cy Young Award ranks second in importance only to the Most Valuable Player Award itself.

Big, strong, and tall, Denton True Young was a farm boy from Tuscarawas County in eastern Ohio. In 1890, when he was 23, the manager of the Canton (Ohio) team in the Tri-State League offered him $40 a month to pitch. The young man's parents were reluctant to give up their son to a career in baseball, because they needed him on the farm. But when the offer was raised to $60 a month, they gave their approval.

At first, the owner of the Canton team was not

Gloves of the 1890s and early 1900s were almost tiny when compared to those in use today. This was the glove used by Cy Young. *(Baseball Hall of Fame)*

very impressed with him. "I thought I had to show him all my stuff," Young once recalled. "I threw the ball so hard I tore up a couple of boards in the grandstand. One of the fellows said it looked like a cyclone struck it. That's how I got the name that was later shortened to Cy."

From the beginning, Cy was a workhorse. He pitched 260 innings in his first professional season for Canton. He had an excellent fastball and a good curve, but it was his control for which he became noted. In his first season, he struck out 201 batters and walked only 33. In the seasons that followed, he sometimes struck out five and six times as many batters as he walked. In 1904, he reached a peak, striking out 203 and walking only 28. As this suggests, Young was a control pitcher, perhaps the best of all time. He had a good fastball and a first-rate curve, but he didn't throw really hard, not by today's standards, anyway.

During his season with Canton, Cy's contract was sold to the Cleveland Spiders of the National League. The next year, his first full season with the club, he appeared in 54 games, won 27 of 47 decisions, and pitched 430 innings. It was the first of 16 seasons—14 in a row—in which he registered 20 or more victories. In five of those seasons, he topped the 30-victory mark. He was to pitching what Babe Ruth was to slugging and Ty Cobb to batting and baserunning.

Cy was able to accomplish all that he did largely because of his amazing endurance. Often he pitched with only two days rest and sometimes with only one. He never complained of having a sore arm, although sometimes he admitted to his arm getting "tired." During the off-season, he kept in shape by performing farm chores, which included plenty of wood chopping.

After 11 seasons with the Cleveland and St. Louis franchises in the National League, Cy switched to the Boston Puritans (later the Red Sox) in the newly established American League. His former employer predicted the league would fail and that Young would go down with it. Of course, the league was a success, and Cy became one of its brightest stars. In each of his first three seasons with Boston, Cy led the American League in victories, winning 33, 32, and 28 games.

Young boasts 511 victories, the most in baseball history. He also has the most defeats—313. *(National Baseball Library)*

Cy Young ended up winning 222 games in the American League and 289 in the National for his total of 511 victories. His 906 game appearances

In 1956, the Cy Young Award was established in Young's honor. *(National Baseball Library)*

stood as the record until broken by relief pitcher Hoyt Wilhelm in 1968. No pitcher has come close to equaling Young's record of 7,377 innings pitched.

How did Cy Young last so long? "I had good arms and legs," he once explained. "When I would go to spring training, I would never touch a ball for three weeks. I just would do a lot of walking and running. I never did any unnecessary throwing. I figured the old arm had just so many throws in it, and there wasn't any use wasting them.

"Like, for instance, I never warmed up ten, fifteen minutes before a game like most pitchers do. I'd loosen up three, four minutes; five, at the most.

"And I never went to the bullpen. Oh, I'd relieve all right, plenty of times, but I went right from the bench to the mound, and I'd take a few warm-up pitches and be ready.

"Then I had good control. I aimed to make the batter hit the ball, and I'd throw as few pitches as possible. That's why I was able to work every other day."

In 1907, at the age of 40, Young won 22 games, lost 15, and pitched six shutouts. The following season, he pitched the third no-hitter of his career, stopping the New York Highlanders, 8–0. Not until Sandy Koufax accomplished that feat nearly 60 years later did anyone hurl three no-hitters. (Koufax eventually posted four no-hitters. Nolan Ryan has seven.) The next year, at 41, Cy posted a 21–11 record.

In Cy's last year with the Puritans, which was 1908, he was honored with a special day at the Huntington Avenue grounds in Boston. There was standing room only, and 20,000 were turned away. Young was given cash gifts that amounted to $6,000, an enormous sum considering his salary never got as high as $5,000 for a season. He also received gifts from a number of opposing players as well as from the league's umpires. Cy was so moved he wasn't able to reply to the speeches delivered in his honor.

In 1909, Young was sold to Cleveland, where he played for three seasons. He won 19 games in 1909, but his record slipped to 7–10 in 1910. After a mediocre start in 1910, Cleveland released him and he signed with the National League's Boston Braves, where he closed out his career. In one of his final appearances with the Braves, Cy was beaten, 1–0, by Grover Cleveland Alexander, then enjoying his rookie season with the Philadelphia Phillies.

When Cy decided to call it quits, his arm was as sound as ever. What he lacked was agility. He had put on a few pounds and batters were bunting on him. "The boys are taking unfair advantage of the old man," he said. "This big stomach of mine makes it difficult to field bunts, so instead of swinging at my pitches, they're laying the ball down."

Once he retired, Cy went back to his farm near Peoli, Ohio. He followed baseball closely and frequently appeared at gatherings of old-timers at major league parks. When Cy turned 80, Bill Veeck, the colorful owner of the Cleveland Indians, held a huge party in his honor and presented him with a new car.

Cy Young died of a heart attack in 1955 at the age of 88, the year before the Cy Young Award was established in his honor. There can be no doubt that if such an award had been around during the years he pitched, Cy Young would have won it many times.

Young retired in 1911. Here he clowns with Nap Lajoie, one of baseball's all-time great hitters, before an old-timers game in Cleveland in 1924. *(both photos Baseball Hall of Fame)*

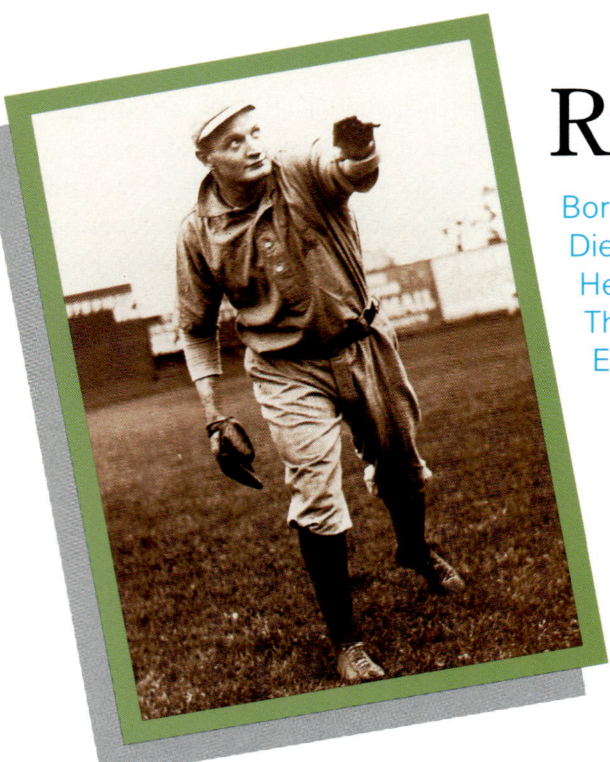

Rube Waddell

Born: October 13, 1876; Bradford, Pennsylvania
Died: April 1, 1914
Height: 6′2″ Weight: 196
Threw left-handed, batted right-handed
Elected to the Hall of Fame in 1946

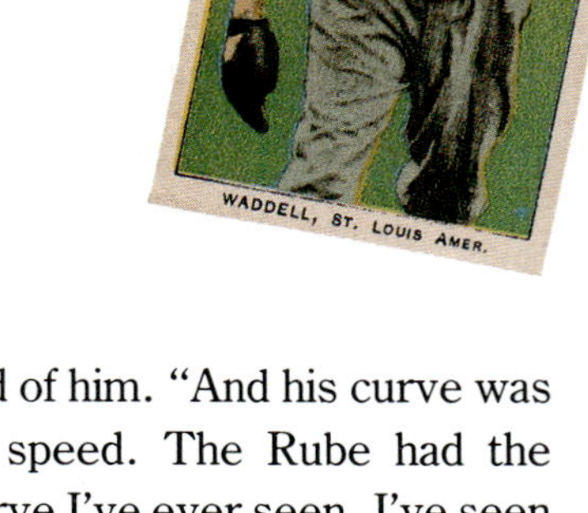

For several seasons during his short career with the Philadelphia Athletics, one of several teams he played for, George Edward ("Rube") Waddell was the best left-handed pitcher in baseball. But he was also a clown and an ordeal for every one of his managers.

Rube once pitched a 17-inning game, hit a triple, and struck out the last three batters. Afterward, he did cartwheels from the mound to the dugout. "He was always laughing out there on the mound," Sam Crawford, a Hall of Fame outfielder for Detroit, once recalled.

Rube was fascinated by fire fighters and never failed to wear a fireman's red shirt under his uniform. He liked to take days off to go fishing or ride fire engines.

A tall and lanky Pennsylvania farm boy, Rube pitched for an assortment of major league teams—Louisville (a National League club in 1908), Pittsburgh, Chicago, Philadelphia, and St. Louis, winning 191 games and losing 142. His best seasons were spent with the Philadelphia Athletics.

"He had terrific speed," Philadelphia manager Connie Mack once said of him. "And his curve was even better than his speed. The Rube had the fastest and deepest curve I've ever seen. I've seen great hitters miss Rube's curve by more than a foot."

Every season from 1902 through 1908, Rube led the American League in strikeouts. Twice during those years he went over the 300 mark.

The season of 1904 was Rube's best in terms of strikeouts. One source says that he struck out 343 batters that year. Another source says it was 349. Because record keeping wasn't done very carefully in those days, nobody knows what the number is for certain. Rube, however, was generally looked upon as the record holder until Sandy Koufax and Nolan Ryan. (Koufax had 382 strikeouts for the Los Angeles Dodgers in 1965; Ryan had 383 strikeouts pitching for the California Angels in 1973.)

Some observers say that 1905 was Rube's greatest season, when he posted a 26–11 record. He easily could have won 30 games that year but he missed the final four weeks of the season (and the World Series, too) because he injured his arm clowning with a teammate in a wrestling match.

It's been written that Waddell, in the late innings of a game, would send his outfielders to the bench, and then proceed to strike out the remaining batters. This could hardly be true, since the rules say that each team must have nine players on the field at all times that they are not at bat. But in exhibition games, Rube would often signal his outfielders to sit down, and then overwhelm the batters, one by one. The crowd loved it.

After his popularity began to decline, the Athletics sold Rube to the St. Louis Browns. He won 19 games for the Browns in 1908, and stuck with the team for a couple more seasons before drifting into the minors.

In 1912, Rube happened to be visiting friends in Hickman, Kentucky, on the Mississippi River, when floods engulfed the area. Rube spent hours in icy waters up to his armpits helping to stack sandbags. The exposure triggered a serious virus infection which led to tuberculosis, a disease that was to take his life two years later.

Rube pitched for Virginia of the Northern League in 1913, winning 3 games and losing 12. But after the season, he was forced to enter a hospital because his condition had so weakened him. He died on April 1, 1914, at the age of 37.

For a period during the years he spent with the Philadelphia Athletics, Waddell was baseball's best left-hander. *(National Baseball Library)*

All-Time Records

Of all the statistical categories that relate to pitching, earned run average is the most important. (The complete name for the statistic is earned run average per nine-inning game.) It is the one statistic for which the pitcher, by his pitching, is wholly responsible. No other reflects a pitcher's effectiveness, or lack of it, so clearly.

To figure a pitcher's earned run average, divide the number of innings pitched into the number of earned runs allowed. This gives the earned runs per inning. Then multiply the result by nine.

Suppose a pitcher, during a season, gave up 91 earned runs in the 238 innings he pitched. Divide the number of innings into the number of earned runs.

```
        .382
238) 91.00
      714
      1960
      1904
        560
        476
```

Then multiply the result by 9.

```
  .382
 x   9
 3.438
```

Earned run average: 3.44

Ed Walsh, one of baseball's early spitball pitchers, has the lowest lifetime earned run average of any pitcher in major league history—1.82. A star performer for the Chicago White Sox during the early 1900s, Big Ed, as he was nicknamed, kept tablets in his mouth made from the inner bark of the slippery elm. These, plus the gum he chewed, helped to provide the saliva he used to "load up" the ball. Walsh would hold his glove in front of his face before each pitch, concealing the ball. Sometimes he would spit on it; sometimes he wouldn't. The batter could only guess whether a spitter was coming.

Walsh, a Hall of Famer, won 195 games during his career. Of course, pitchers today aren't permitted to throw spitters or doctor the ball in any way.

Early pitchers, from the standpoint of their ERAs, at least, also benefited from the fact that baseball, in the first two decades of the century, was a relatively low-scoring game. Not until the 1920s did Babe Ruth, then others, really start to slug the ball.

To qualify as the earned run champion for a season, a pitcher must work at least the same number of innings as games on the schedule—162 in the American and National Leagues.

EARNED RUN AVERAGE

1	Ed Walsh	1.82
2	Addie Joss	1.89
3	Mordecai Brown	2.06
4	Monte Ward	2.10
5	Christy Mathewson	2.13
6	Rube Waddell	2.16
7	Walter Johnson	2.17
8	Orval Overall	2.24
9	Tommy Bond	2.25
10	Ed Reulbach	2.28
	Will White	2.28
12	Jim Scott	2.30
13	Eddie Plank	2.35
14	Larry Corcoran	2.36
15	Eddie Cicotte	2.38
	Ed Killian	2.38
	George McQuillan	2.38
18	Doc White	2.39
19	Nap Rucker	2.42
20	Terry Larkin	2.43
	Jim McCormick	2.43
	Jeff Tesreau	2.43
23	Chief Bender	2.46
24	Sam Leever	2.47
	Hooks Wiltse	2.47

WINS

1	Cy Young	511
2	Walter Johnson	416
3	Grover Cleveland Alexander	373
	Christy Mathewson	373
5	Warren Spahn	363
6	Kid Nichols	361
7	Jim Galvin	360
8	Tim Keefe	342
9	Steve Carlton	329
10	John Clarkson	328
11	Eddie Plank	326
12	Don Sutton	324
13	Nolan Ryan*	319
14	Phil Niekro	318
15	Gaylord Perry	314
16	Tom Seaver	311
17	Charles Radbourn	309
18	Mickey Welch	307
19	Lefty Grove	300
	Early Wynn	300
21	Tommy John	288
22	Bert Blyleven*	287
23	Robin Roberts	286
24	Ferguson Jenkins	284
	Tony Mullane	284

* Still active, 1993

SHUTOUTS

1	Walter Johnson	110
2	Grover Cleveland Alexander	90
3	Christy Mathewson	79
4	Cy Young	76
5	Eddie Plank	69
6	Warren Spahn	63
7	Nolan Ryan*	61
	Tom Seaver	61
9	Bert Blyleven*	60
10	Don Sutton	58
11	Ed Walsh	57
12	Jim Galvin	56
	Bob Gibson	56
14	Mordecai Brown	55
	Steve Carlton	55
16	Jim Palmer	53
	Gaylord Perry	53
18	Juan Marichal	52
19	Rube Waddell	50
	Vic Willis	50
21	Don Drysdale	49
	Ferguson Jenkins	49
	Luis Tiant	49
	Early Wynn	49
25	Kid Nichols	48

*Still active, 1993

STRIKEOUTS

1	Nolan Ryan*	5,668
2	Steve Carlton	4,136
3	Bert Blyleven*	3,701
4	Tom Seaver	3,640
5	Don Sutton	3,574
6	Gaylord Perry	3,534
7	Walter Johnson	3,508
8	Phil Niekro	3,342
9	Ferguson Jenkins	3,192
10	Bob Gibson	3,117
11	Jim Bunning	2,855
12	Mickey Lolich	2,832
13	Cy Young	2,800
14	Frank Tanana*	2,657
15	Warren Spahn	2,583
16	Bob Feller	2,581
17	Jerry Koosman	2,556
18	Tim Keefe	2,527
19	Christy Mathewson	2,502
20	Don Drysdale	2,486
21	Jim Kaat	2,461
22	Sam McDowell	2,453
23	Luis Tiant	2,416
24	Sandy Koufax	2,396
25	Robin Roberts	2,357

*Still active, 1993

BASES ON BALLS

1	Nolan Ryan*	2,755
2	Steve Carlton	1,833
3	Phil Niekro	1,809
4	Early Wynn	1,775
5	Bob Feller	1,764
6	Bobo Newsom	1,732
7	Amos Rusie	1,704
8	Gus Weyhing	1,566
9	Charlie Hough*	1,542
10	Red Ruffing	1,541
11	Bump Hadley	1,442
12	Warren Spahn	1,434
13	Earl Whitehill	1,431
14	Tony Mullane	1,408
15	Sam Jones	1,396
16	Tom Seaver	1,390
17	Gaylord Perry	1,379
18	Mike Torrez	1,371
19	Walter Johnson	1,362
20	Don Sutton	1,343
21	Bob Gibson	1,336
22	Chick Fraser	1,332
23	Bert Blyleven*	1,322
24	Sam McDowell	1,312
25	Jim Palmer	1,311

* Still active, 1993

COMPLETE GAMES

1	Cy Young	749
2	Jim Galvin	639
3	Tim Keefe	554
4	Walter Johnson	531
	Kid Nichols	531
6	Mickey Welch	525
7	Charles Radbourn	489
8	John Clarkson	485
9	Tony Mullane	468
10	Jim McCormick	466
11	Gus Weyhing	448
12	Grover Cleveland Alexander	438
13	Christy Mathewson	434
14	Jack Powell	422
15	Eddie Plank	410
16	Will White	394
17	Amos Rusie	392
18	Vic Willis	388
19	Warren Spahn	382
20	Jim Whitney	377
21	Adonis Terry	367
22	Ted Lyons	356
23	George Mullin	353
24	Charlie Buffinton	351
25	Chick Fraser	342

GAMES

1	Hoyt Wilhelm	1,070
2	Kent Tekulve	1,050
3	Lindy McDaniel	987
4	Rollie Fingers	944
5	Gene Garber	931
6	Rich Gossage*	927
7	Cy Young	906
8	Sparky Lyle	899
9	Jim Kaat	898
10	Don McMahon	874
11	Phil Niekro	864
12	Roy Face	848
13	Tug McGraw	824
14	Charlie Hough*	803
15	Walter Johnson	802
16	Nolan Ryan*	794
17	Gaylord Perry	777
18	Don Sutton	774
19	Darold Knowles	765
20	Tommy John	760
21	Jack Quinn	756
22	Ron Reed	751
23	Warren Spahn	750
24	Tom Burgmeier	745
	Gary Lavelle	745

* Still active, 1993

WINNERS OF 300 GAMES

Pitcher	Team/League	Date	Total Career Wins
Nolan Ryan*	Texas (American League)	July 31, 1990	319
Don Sutton	California (American League)	June 18, 1986	324
Phil Niekro	New York (American League)	Oct. 6, 1985	318
Tom Seaver	Chicago (American League)	Aug. 4, 1985	311
Steve Carlton	Philadelphia (National League)	Sept. 23, 1983	329
Gaylord Perry	Seattle (American League)	May 6, 1982	314
Early Wynn	Cleveland (American League)	July 13, 1963	300
Warren Spahn	Milwaukee (National League)	Aug. 11, 1961	363
Lefty Grove	Boston (American League)	July 25, 1941	300
Grover Cleveland Alexander	Chicago (National League)	Sept. 20, 1924	373
Walter Johnson	Washington (American League)	May 29, 1920	416
Eddie Plank	St. Louis (Federal League)	Aug. 11, 1915	326
Christy Mathewson	New York (National League)	July 5, 1912	373
Cy Young	Boston (American League)	July 6, 1901	511
Kid Nichols	Boston (National League)	June 13, 1900	361
John Clarkson	Cleveland (National League)	Sept. 21, 1892	328
Charles Radbourn	Cincinnati (National League)	June 2, 1891	309
Mickey Welch	New York (National League)	July 28, 1890	307
Tim Keefe	New York (Players League)	June 4, 1890	342
Jim Galvin	Pittsburgh (National League)	Sept. 29, 1888	360

*Still active, 1993

LOSSES

Rank	Pitcher	Losses
1	Cy Young	316
2	Jim Galvin	308
3	Nolan Ryan*	287
4	Walter Johnson	279
5	Phil Niekro	274
6	Gaylord Perry	265
7	Don Sutton	256
8	Jack Powell	254
9	Eppa Rixey	251
10	Bert Blyleven*	250
11	Robin Roberts	245
	Warren Spahn	245
13	Steve Carlton	244
	Early Wynn	244
15	Jim Kaat	237
16	Gus Weyhing	232
17	Tommy John	231
18	Bob Friend	230
	Ted Lyons	230
20	Ferguson Jenkins	226
21	Tim Keefe	225
	Red Ruffing	225
23	Bobo Newsom	222
24	Tony Mullane	220
25	Jack Quinn	218

* Still active, 1993

Index

Note: Numbers in italics indicate picture captions.